The Man
Who Walked
Through
Walls

The Man Who Walked Through Walls

James Swain

St. Martin's Press/New York

THE MAN WHO WALKED THROUGH WALLS. Copyright © 1989 by James Swain.
All rights reserved. Printed in the United States of America. No part of this
book may be used or reproduced in any manner whatsoever without written
permission except in the case of brief quotations embodied in critical articles
or reviews. For information, address St. Martin's Press, 175 Fifth Avenue,
New York, N.Y. 10010.

Library of Congress Cataloging-in-Publication Data

Swain, James.
  The man who walked through walls.
    p. cm.
  "A Thomas Dunne book."
  ISBN 0-312-03394-X
  I. Title.
PS3569.W225M36 1989   813'.54—dc20   89-33028

First Edition
10 9 8 7 6 5 4 3 2 1

To my parents,
with love

The Music Hall where I was playing was packed, and while watching me became fairly wild. I kept on, but I was only about half conscious. Every joint in my body was aching, and I had but little use of my arms. I asked as a favor that he free my hands long enough for the circulation to start again, but he only laughed and exclaimed, "This is no love affair, this is a contest. Say you are defeated and I'll release you."

I gritted my teeth and went at it once more. For two hours and a half I exerted myself, fighting for my professional good name. In the meanwhile, the audience was cheering itself hoarse. Some cried "Give it up," and others, "Keep on, you'll do it." I don't believe any such scene was ever acted in a theater. The house was crazy with excitement, and I was covered with blood brought on by my exertion to release myself and chafing irons. But I did it. I got free of every chain and handcuff. Then they had to carry me off stage, and I suffered from the effects for months afterwards.

—Harry Houdini

Author's Note

All of the magic used in *The Man Who Walked Through Walls* is based on real tricks, illusions, and escapes used by professional magicians. I have carefully avoided exposing anything that cannot be found in your basic library magic book. The shark escape has never been performed, but the method I used would indeed be workable, and includes principles that Houdini used in several of his escapes.

The Houdini Museum is located in Niagara Falls, Canada, and there is a small strongbox that contains the fabled Houdini Secret. No one claims to know what the secret is; however, I learned several years ago from one of Houdini's biographers that a device like the one I describe was discovered in the attic of the escape artist's old home in New York, and many people believe it was the foundation for a number of Houdini's more miraculous impromptu escapes.

*The Man
Who Walked
Through
Walls*

Chapter 1

The London Palladium

*L*adies and gentlemen, for our next act this evening, I would like to introduce a very unusual man." Microphone in hand, master of ceremonies Sir Paul Cromford moved downstage. "His name, Vincent Hardare. Tonight marks the anniversary of his uncle Harry Houdini's first engagement in London. Allow me to present the rightful heir of Houdini, master of the impossible—Hardare."

The house lights dimmed, the curtains rising to the strains of a showy Gershwin tune. The mammoth, cen-

1

tury-old Palladium stage was empty, void of the glitzy props and jiggling half-dressed girls that marred most magic acts. Suddenly a brilliant flash of fire lit up center stage, and from the resulting puff of smoke emerged a man elegantly attired in white tie and tails. The sold-out house, consisting mostly of dignitaries and London's upper crust, applauded enthusiastically, the magician's face instantly recognizable to anyone who read the newspapers or owned a television set. Hardare's highly publicized escapes—his most recent from a house packed with explosives—had made his name synonymous with getting out of tight situations, and the expression "To do a Hardare" had become a popular euphemism when trying to convey the idea of the truly impossible.

For a long moment, Vincent Hardare stood in the spotlight, beaming. Fifteen years of hard work had brought him here, and for the briefest moment he was going to be selfish, and bathe himself in applause. His uncle, Harry Houdini, had made his reputation in London after having worked second-rate vaudeville houses and circuses in America for ten years, and Hardare did not think the additional five years it had taken himself to reach this plateau was too much to ask, not when he considered the rewards.

"Thank you and good evening," he said into the microphone. "Tonight, as a tribute to Houdini, I would like to perform two of his famous and most cherished routines. The first, the unique de Kolta die."

A stunning brunette in a strapless black chiffon evening dress pushed a wheeled platform out beside him. She grinned at him, and Hardare winked at her. He wondered how enjoyable any of this would be without

2

his wife Barbara by his side, and found the thought almost incomprehensible.

Sitting on the platform was one of a pair of black-and-white dice, the size of a soccer ball. Solid in appearance, it was actually constructed of unbelievably strong telescopic rods covered with expandable Chinese silk. Among magic collectors, it was valued as a priceless treasure, and Hardare had kept it in storage for years, knowing that the trick could only be performed a few more times before the rods would stop working. "The de Kolta die was Houdini's favorite illusion," he said, tossing the object cautiously from hand to hand, "and a favorite of audiences around the world. Watch carefully. Blink once, and the illusion is lost forever." Setting the die down, he hooked his thumb into a hidden wire loop on back. "What is an illusion? A trick of the eye or the mind. You be the judge."

Hardare set the die back on the platform, then spied the orchestra leader tapping his baton. During dress rehearsals that afternoon the orchestra leader had become so absorbed trying to figure the trick out, he had completely forgotten his cue, and they had been forced to start over. This time the drum roll started when it was supposed to. Raising his arms dramatically, Hardare tugged at the wire loop, triggering the die's hidden telescopic rods. There was a clash of cymbals.

The audience emitted a collective gasp. The die had instantly expanded into an enormous six-foot cube, completely filling the small stand. The effect was so startling that it took several moments to register, and the applause, which was at first scattered, quickly grew into a nice ovation.

From stage left appeared a blonde fourteen-year-

3

old girl wearing a dress identical to her mother's. Hardare extended his hand to her, and she joined him in the middle of the stage.

"When Houdini performed the de Kolta die, his wife Bess acted as his assistant," Hardare said. "Please allow me to introduce my daughter, Crystal."

There was more applause, and Crystal smiled shyly, afraid the bright spotlight would reflect off her braces. Hardare lifted the die from the platform, allowing the audience to see its hollow interior. His daughter sat on the platform cross-legged, and Hardare placed the die completely over her.

Then he stepped forward, clapping his hands together dramatically. "Perhaps you are wondering why this trick was a favorite of Houdini's. Well, my uncle loved surprises. And so do I. Here, let me show you."

Stepping back, Hardare lifted the die into the air, and the cymbals clashed again. He heard a chorus of gasps. There, on the platform, sitting beneath the hollow die, was Sheba, a snarling three-hundred-pound Bengal tiger. His daughter was nowhere—gone. The audience responded by bursting into applause, and Sheba let out a roar to raise the rafters. Hardare felt the air rush from his lungs; he had completely fooled them. He could think of no greater exhilaration in the world.

A trainer escorted Sheba offstage. The first routine was always the biggest hurdle, and Hardare felt himself warming to the packed house. The Royal Variety Show was an annual event in London, regularly attended by the Royal Family and their distinguished guests. The show was also televised, and Hardare had rented an empty hall and rehearsed for a week, knowing that even at this lofty stage of his career, he could not afford to botch a trick or suffer an accident on stage.

"That's one assistant I won't argue with." Smiling, he stepped to the footlights as the curtains closed.

"Within a year of his first London show," Hardare told the audience, "Houdini was a sensation throughout Europe. But his success spawned many imitators. One was an escape artist named David Hardare. Like Houdini, Hardare was young, brash, and an American.

"The two men quickly became rivals. Often they appeared in neighboring cities, and issued public challenges to each other. Their feuding lasted many years. Only after Houdini's untimely death in 1926 did Hardare tell the world the truth. He and Houdini were brothers. Their rivalry was nothing more than a clever publicity stunt that Houdini had concocted years before.

"During their lives, the brothers exchanged many tricks and ideas. The following escape was a personal favorite in both Houdini's and my father's act."

The curtains rose. A thick black rope hung in center stage. Beside it stood two men in prison gray uniforms holding a canvas straitjacket between them. Squinting into the bright spotlight, one of them loudly whispered, "Look, Barney, up in the balcony. It's the bleedin' Queen."

"These two gentlemen work the mental ward of a local hospital," Hardare said. "Please identify yourselves."

"Name's Barney Codd," the first volunteered.

"Harold Pickwick," the second offered, still gaping up at his sovereign.

With their help, Hardare displayed the straitjacket.

"Houdini loved a challenge. Escaping from a strait-jacket is hard enough, almost impossible while hanging upside down. When Houdini first tried this difficult feat, it took him ten minutes. Later, my father cut the time in half. Tonight, hanging by my ankles, I will escape in two minutes—or pay the penalty for failure."

Hardare directed the audience's attention to a dark-ened section of the rope. "For the past hour, this rope has been soaked in gasoline. When lit, it will burn through in two minutes. If I fail to escape in time, the rope will break, and I will fall headfirst to the stage."

Murmurs filled the house. The hint of tragedy had a titillating effect on even the most sophisticated crowd. The mood had been set, and while a stagehand attached a block and tackle to the rope, Hardare removed his cutaway jacket, and let Codd and Pickwick fit him into the canvas restraining device.

The two were strong men, and working silently, they tugged and jerked Hardare around the giant stage, securing the leather straps tautly across his back. Their effort was a show in itself, and with each powerful tug Hardare emitted an audible grunt. Unknown to Codd and Pickwick, he had filled his lungs with air, and ex-panded his chest an additional four inches, a feat most bodybuilders would have envied. For his purposes, it let him obtain slack inside the jacket no matter how snugly it was fitted. Like so many impressive escapes, the secret was relatively simple; Hardare simply made his body bigger.

Codd tapped his shoulder. "Hope you can breathe."

Hardare stepped to the mike. "In a few moments

I will be hoisted into the air, and the rope set afire. Sir Paul Cromford will act as our official timekeeper. Please wish me luck."

The performer's assistant attached the rope to his ankles, then held him steady as a motor drew the rope up through a pulley in the ceiling. Hardare went into the air feet first, and whispered to his assistant, "Hold me tight, John."

He wondered if anyone in the audience appreciated the risk he was taking. Months ago he had seen an ambitious English boy named Bernard perform an outdoor straitjacket while hanging upside down from a helicopter. The wind had picked up, and when the chopper dipped, Bernard's head snapped against the pavement. The crowd had quickly dispersed, not interested in grisly aftermaths. At the boy's funeral, Hardare had acted as a pallbearer, and later, learning the family was broke, paid for a tombstone. *This could be you*, he had thought, watching the stone being placed on the fresh grave. It had depressed him for weeks.

When he was five feet up, the motor stopped. John held the mike up to him and he said, "Ladies and gentlemen, in two minutes I will return to the stage, one way or another." He smiled, heard laughter. "Ready, Sir Paul?"

"Ready," Cromford replied, stopwatch in hand.

"Then let's go!"

The mike was removed. From the wings, Barbara made her appearance holding a long torch. She allowed the flame to lick the darkened section of rope, igniting the gasoline, and Hardare was immediately raised another few feet.

"Knock them dead, Vincent," she whispered.

7

She gave him a little smile and walked off. Hardare closed his eyes and let his body twirl. There were certain aspects about working with his wife that he did not enjoy. Especially if she was worried over a difficult new escape—like tonight's—or if something had fouled up at rehearsal. Sometimes it made it hard knowing she was standing off in the wings, turning a Kleenex into confetti, watching him.

"Thirty seconds," Sir Paul announced.

Hardare blew out his lungs and shrunk his chest. His arms loosened, and he began to spin faster and faster, the sparks flying across the stage. Codd and Pickwick ran for cover while the orchestra played a rousing selection by Tchaikovsky. By dislocating both his shoulders, Hardare slowly brought his arms over his head.

"One minute," Sir Paul cautioned.

Working his fingers through the stiff canvas, he undid the leather straps on his back one by one. By now he was soaked with perspiration and every muscle in his body ached. *Pick it up*, he thought, growing dizzier by the second. The jacket gradually started to come undone. He was almost home.

"A minute and a half."

At this point he was essentially free. Years of practice had honed the straitjacket escape down to ninety seconds. The extra thirty seconds he allowed himself was insurance against anything going wrong—a necessary allotment, since Lloyd's of London refused to issue him a policy.

A drum roll. Time for the new, show-stopping addition to his act. Above him, implanted in the block and tackle, was a cylinder containing a highly pressurized phosphorescent charge. He slowly counted to five.

"One minute forty—!"

That was their cue. Standing offstage, John activated a transmitter that opened the cylinder, and set Hardare's wildly spinning body into bright orange flames. He looked like a nova, and up in the balcony, an impressionable woman shrieked. Hardare heard her, and with eyes tightly shut thought, *Keep it up, honey*.

The stage went black; only the orange lights could be seen. He heard more shrieks, men's yells. The same thing had happened at dress rehearsal that afternoon; no one had known if it was part of the act, or a horrible accident. And the darkness only made it worse . . .

He had exactly four seconds. Throwing off the smoking jacket, he doubled his body, releasing himself from the block and tackle, and jumped to the darkened stage. Landing in a crouch, his hands touched the sooty floor, and helped propel him to a standing position as a spotlight immediately enveloped him.

Happy to see him alive, the audience burst into applause. Hardare raised his right fist triumphantly in the air. "Ladies and gentlemen," he heard Sir Paul boom, "the amazing Hardare. Well done, sir. Well done." The ovation continued. He took a bow, and behind him the block and tackle crashed to the stage: the penalty for failure. Then his wife and daughter joined him on stage. The applause intensified, and for a heart-warming minute the audience refused to let them go. Remembering their instructions, the family bowed to the Royal Box. From the balcony someone yelled "Bravo," and for a fleeting instant he felt absolutely euphoric. He squeezed his daughter and Barbara's hand, and when the curtains closed, kissed his wife on the lips.

Chapter 2

Acapulco, Two Years Later

S mashed on half a pint of Cuervo Gold, Crystal Hardare teetered precariously on the lip of a third floor balcony overlooking the kidney-shaped hotel swimming pool far below. Shouts came through an open window on the second floor, her classmates engaged in a raucous game of Yahtzee. *What are you trying to prove?* she wondered drunkenly. None of her friends were watching, or could help if she got seriously hurt. She shrugged it off; if she busted a leg or cracked open her skull, well, shit happens, even on vacation.

11

A month after the accident that killed her mother, Crystal and her dad had moved to London. He wanted to get away, and England was the best place, since he had once performed for the Queen, and that helped him get bookings there. At first the change was good. They rented a townhouse in the West End, went to shows, cooked together, and on Sunday afternoons watched jugglers and mimes and ranting Communists on soapboxes in Hyde Park. One Sunday, after buying ice cream, her dad had said, "Your mom is gone, but we shouldn't let her spirit die. Let's live our lives a day at a time, and stop brooding about the past. She would have liked that." Crystal had understood; she cried and ate her cone. Later they had a Chinese dinner and saw a movie, and she'd felt a little better.

But it didn't last. For her dad, working in England was different than in the United States. Instead of performing a few months in a hotel or nightclub, acts worked one week here, one week there. Hardare soon exhausted the London clubs and, having grown sick of touring the provinces and living out of a suitcase, began accepting extended bookings in Paris, Amsterdam, and Madrid. They were constantly on the road, and in each new city Crystal had attended a new school, with new teachers and kids with funny last names. She was always an outsider, always behind in her classes, and at night, instead of trying to catch up, she started following her father to the clubs. She hung around backstage doing odd jobs and smoking cigarettes with the makeup girls and stagehands. She was soon pulling Ds, and one day she simply decided to drop out, but made the fatal mistake of first telling her dad.

He had read the riot act to her. She was going to

stay in school, graduate, one day have a career. Her mother would have wanted it that way. "Leave her out of it!" Crystal had shouted at him. "Her vote doesn't count anymore!"

In anger, Hardare had threatened to send her away. Her aunt was still good friends with the director of admissions at Rosemary Hall, the prestigious girl's boarding school in Connecticut. It would only take a phone call. Just try it, Crystal had dared him, slamming a bedroom door in his face. Just watch, he had said through the door.

Fuck him, she'd said to herself so many times since leaving Europe. *Fuck him*. Rosemary Hall was dull; no one took chances. Her classmates were rich and hopelessly spoiled. They already knew which colleges they were going to, and what their careers would be. *Fuck them*, she'd said as many times, then had cut a class or broken curfew and left her dormitory late at night. *Just fuck them one good time, once and for all.*

Crystal got set, yelled "Geronimo!" and jumped.

It was a long, terrifying drop, but she hit the pool's deep end and leveled out before touching bottom. Jumping gave her a tremendous rush of adrenalin, and she decided to go again.

As her head broke the surface, she heard a man's anguished scream, and Crystal stood on the short grass surrounding the pool trying to discern where the man was. Each room of the Torreblanco Hotel had a spacious balcony, half of them facing the pool, the others looking down on the clogged streets of touristy Puerto Marques. The scream had silenced the building, and for a moment she could hear herself breathing, the deep inhalations little comfort to her already pounding heart.

13

Perhaps it was a car, or a TV turned on full blast. Whatever it was, it was not repeated, and in its place had begun a wild water balloon fight on the fourth and fifth floor balconies. Crystal hurried back inside.

As Maria Alvarez walked through the front doors of the Torreblanco Hotel, she wondered if this was the start of a new life. No more midnight rendezvous, or dropping secret messages in prearranged spots; no more carrying guns, or looking behind you when you drove. Her assignment was finished, and to hell with what her superiors said. She and Miguel were heading for that seaside cottage near Juchitan, where Miguel would manage the restaurant he'd talked about for years—"The other thing I want beside you," he'd whispered the night before after their lovemaking. She would be his *cocinera*, preparing the ancient Mayan delicacies her grandmother had passed down to her when she was a child.

Inside the hotel nightclub a steel band was playing mariachi; the catchy tune followed her across the lobby, which was mobbed with a tour group of Canadians wearing straw hats and drinking out of paper cups. She caught the eye of an older cashier working the front desk. He found her room key and gave her a toothy smile. When she was in an elevator heading upstairs, he picked up a house phone.

"She just walked in."

On the fifth floor Maria passed her room twice to make sure she hadn't been followed. She unlocked the door, calling Miguel's name softly. When he did not respond, she stiffened and chained the door behind her. A nightlight beside the bed was on, and on the table a vase of long stem red roses. A small object winked at her from the floor beside the bed. She picked it up.

It was a small opal ring, oddly familar except for the color, which seemed to change from green to blue each time she turned it over on her palm. She slipped it on her third finger. It was Miguel's.

What did it mean? She took the ring off, and holding it close to her eyes, saw a dark crust edging the stone. She scraped it off with her fingernail. She pressed it between her fingers and it disintegrated into dust.

Maria heard playful screams. Opening the doors to the balcony overlooking the pool, she stepped outside. One floor below a demented blonde girl—no doubt part of the invasion of American teenagers in the hotel—was jumping from one balcony railing to the next with the agility of a circus acrobat.

Maria heard a loud rap on her door. "Room service."

"I didn't order any," she called into the room. A shoulder splintered the door. She fumbled with her purse, looking for her gun, as two burly men wearing turtlenecks and navy blue sports coats burst in. She saw the revolvers in their hands, then their faces. Not men, *wolves.* "Bastards!" she cried. Climbing over the balcony railing, she jumped.

She landed on all fours on the balcony directly below, stood, felt her ankle scream, went back down. Suddenly she realized her pocketbook was gone, and gazed through the railing at the dense hedge encircling the hotel pool. She supposed it was as safe a place as any to hide it.

"Hey, lady," Crystal called from the adjacent balcony. "Did you hurt yourself?"

"Please—don't come . . ." but Crystal had already made another heroic leap, and climbed the railing beside her. "There are men chasing me," Maria cried. "Trying to kill me."

"No shit?" Crystal replied, belching tequila in Maria's face. Holding the girl's arm, Maria managed to stand on rubbery legs, and noticed that Crystal's hair and clothes were soaking wet.

Suddenly a water balloon burst between them, making Maria jump back in fear. Again her ankle screamed. "Be careful," Crystal said. "The red ones are filled with piss."

"Hey, Hardare, you snake," a drunken girl hollered from the balcony above. "This one's got your name on it!"

Another balloon sailed by. "Listen, lady," Crystal said. "I've got to beat it."

Maria clutched her arm desperately. "No! Call hotel security. Tell them—"

"Are you serious? Those bozos want to throw me out of the hotel." She slipped out of Maria's grasp as if slipping off a blouse. "It's been a blast. Stay in touch," and climbing the railing, jumped to the adjacent balcony, then the next, finally disappearing through the doors of an open room.

Maria tried to follow. The slightest pressure on her ankle was agonizing. She sagged against the railing. It was no good; she'd only fall and kill herself. She heard the balcony's doors open, and turned to watch her pursuers slip noiselessly outside. Guns drawn, they made her back away from the railing. She did as told and nervously fingered her lover's opal ring. Perhaps they would soon be together again.

"Where is your pocketbook?" asked the gunman on her left.

"In a safe place," she whispered.

"We can make you talk," he threatened, bringing the barrel of his gun to within inches of her quivering lips.

"I . . ." Maria glanced up, then bit her tongue, knowing if she laughed in his face he'd make her pay dearly later on. The gunman hesitated, then looked straight up at the balcony above them, his knees buckling as the perfectly aimed red balloon splattered on his forehead.

Maria screamed into the knotted sock. Sharp-edged waves of agony rippled through her body. She was back in her room, naked, tied to the four-poster bed she and Miguel had shared the night before. The knife touched her skin again, and she began to ascend, her soul ready to float up through the ceiling, when a black cloud swept over her, plunging into a pool of darkness. In her delirium, she saw Miguel standing beside the bed. He was naked, too, and smiling at her. He extended his hand.

She awoke to consciousness a minute later, hot and drenched with sweat. Rafael Guerra stared down at her impassively. He was dressed in his faded camel-colored uniform and still looked as innocent and as handsome as a young altar boy. Holding a stiletto over a burning candle, he let the tip turn a glowing reddish-orange.

"Your boyfriend wanted you to have the roses,"

Guerra said. He gently undid the gag. "I don't think you deserve to die the way he did. Earlier tonight you broke into my office and stole a list of names. My men followed you, yet still you managed to get rid of the information. But to whom? Tell me who your contact is, and I will spare you."

There *was* no name, but what would telling him the truth bring? It was hard to believe he'd be merciful, and wouldn't simply slit her throat. His depravity had too many dimensions; he would use his gun hand with her first, play with her vagina, try to make her cry until she was to the point of hysteria. *Then* he'd kill her.

"I dropped my pocketbook down the laundry chute in the hall," she said, her mind working furiously. "A man was waiting in the basement. He hired me to rob you. I don't know his name. He was an American, wearing a seersucker suit."

"Cunt liar," intoned the gunman standing beside Guerra, his hair still wet from his inadvertent shower. "You had that purse in your hand when you jumped over the balcony. I saw you." He pinched Maria's left nipple between his thumb and forefinger as if it were a loose button he wanted to tear off.

"Why won't you tell me the truth?" Guerra said, brushing an errant strand of hair from her face.

"I swear on my mother's grave," Maria said, hardly able to speak. "Believe me. Please."

Guerra glanced at the other gunman, who sat at the foot of the bed staring longingly between Maria's legs. "Carlos, you're a good judge of character. What do you think?" Without averting his eyes, Carlos grunted negatively. "I think you're right," Guerra said, picking up the stiletto. With a surgeon's precision, he placed the tip beneath her throat and drew a perfect straight line between her breasts down to her navel.

It felt no different than a feather, and Maria watched the blood swell and ooze down to her pubic hairs. Fear swept over her, a destructive agent greater than the most excruciating pain. She heard herself let out a sob.

"The name, Maria."

The names of dozens of people she wouldn't mind seeing dead flashed through her mind. But how much time could she buy? A day, perhaps two. The ending was still the same. "There was no contact," she finally admitted. "I was working alone."

"Hardare," said the wet-haired gunman. "There was a young blonde on the balcony, an American. A girl above called out her name. *Hardare.* I heard it clearly."

"No!" Maria insisted, seeing it register in Guerra's eyes. "The girl has nothing to do with this. She saw me fall, helped me up—"

"Took your pocketbook," Guerra said.

"No . . . I dropped it," she said.

"Thank you, Maria," he said, tightly re-doing the gag. Before he had finished, Carlos had taken a towel and wiped away Maria's blood. Then he stripped off his own clothes and climbed atop her helpless, squirming body.

For a minute Guerra stood by the four-poster and observed their muted coupling. Carlos, his hairy back dotted with sweat, was grunting loudly with each pelvic thrust while Maria lay impassively beneath him, her eyes tightly shut. It was like watching a gorilla with a corpse, and he went outside on the balcony to smoke a cigarette.

The cigarette helped him think. The explanation was ridiculous enough to be true. Someone had been passing information in front of their noses for a year, and he had never suspected it might be a kid, or someone who looked like a kid. But something didn't sit right. Perhaps it was the girl's name. *Hardare.* Years ago in an Acapulco movie house packed with drunks and hysterical women, he had watched as on the screen a man named Hardare jumped out of an airplane, his arms triple-handcuffed behind him. A man with a portable camera jumped with him, recording every movement, and Hardare had dramatically opened the final pair of cuffs and pulled the ripcord on his parachute with only seconds to spare. The audience had gone wild, and Guerra had angrily pushed his way to an exit, convinced it was a colossal fraud. Later, reeling drunk and lying in bed with a whore, he had come to an altogether different conclusion, and decided it was perhaps the bravest thing he'd ever seen.

And it would be typical of the DEA to use someone as unsuspecting as a teenage girl. They often used women in their undercover operations—prostitutes, and idealistic young Mexican girls that they recruited from the colleges.

Guerra went back inside. Naked, Raul stood by the bed, dutifully waiting his turn.

"Raul," Guerra said, "Go downstairs and see if this Hardare girl is registered in the hotel. Or still running around."

Maria's eyes were still closed, her head turned side-

20

ways on the pillow. Raul grabbed his erection with his hand. "Carlos gets laid, and I get this. Shit." He tugged on his pants begrudgingly. "What if she recognizes me, and gives me trouble?"

"I want her unharmed," he said, noticing the crust of cocaine edging Raul's left nostril. "Arrest her. After all, you are a policeman."

"On what charge?"

"Make one fucking up," Guerra replied.

Jumping into the pool a second time, Crystal kept her eyes wide open, watching until the last possible moment as the illuminated water rushed up to catch her. It was a blue net, only warm and friendly, the air bubbles bursting in her ears like applause.

Crystal resurfaced immediately and saw a man standing beside the pool. She climbed out, shook herself dry, and stared up into the face of a beefy Wayne Newton clone. "Are you hotel security?"

He showed her a shiny silver badge. "Police. You are under arrest."

"Say what? Hey! Get your hands off me! Help. . . !"

Ignoring her screams, he dragged her into a darkened alley beside the hotel, handcuffed her wrists together, and threw her into the back of a white Eldorado with the engine running, then jumped into the front as the car sped off.

"What are you doing to me?" she screamed.

"Do not be frightened," said a voice beside her.

Lifting her face off the leather seat, Crystal stared

into the olive-colored face of the most handsome man she'd ever seen, even in his drab police uniform. He smiled grimly and her fear melted into tears. "I haven't done anything wrong," she protested, swallowing a sob. "This isn't right. Who are you?"

"Keep your mouth shut," he said, turning his head away.

The car raced through the busy downtown, ignoring stop signs and traffic lights, sending pedestrians scurrying for cover. Up front, sandwiched between the driver and Wayne Newton, there was a woman in a bathrobe. She seemed to be unconscious. Her mouth was covered with masking tape. She looked drugged and Crystal thought, *I've got to get back to the hotel, find one of the chaperones.*

They took a corner on two wheels, and Crystal used the distraction to raise her handcuffs and peer into the keyhole. It was a regulation pair, nothing fancy. As a twelve-year-old she had earned her allowance by picking the locks of handcuffs from her dad's vast collection, twenty-five cents a pop. Taking a bobby pin from her hair, she bent a hook in one end, and found the release spring on the first try. Both cuffs popped open easily.

She had the cuffs off when the car screeched to a halt in front of a brick fortress with bars on the windows. She relocked both halves of the cuffs over her right fist, making a gauntlet.

Her handsome captor got out, motioning for her to follow. Crystal stepped after him, touched pavement, and swung at the first man to lay his hands on her. Her fist sunk into the loose fold of flesh above Wayne Newton's beltline, and he collapsed into the gutter, making retching noises.

She started to run, and Handsome was instantly on top of her. He tried to grab her arm, and she planted her feet the way she'd learned in self-defense class, and threw a looping right at his head. He ducked beneath it. Suddenly his eyes went very wide.

"Your handcuffs—how did you open them?" A knowledgeable look spread across his face. "I was right. Your father is the escape artist, the amazing Hardare."

His thin lips formed into a smile. Crystal hesitated, her fist cocked by her side. The front doors of the police station burst open, and a dozen armed officers piled out and formed a tight circle around them. Crystal began to shudder uncontrollably. Seeing this, Guerra barked out an order in Spanish, and all of the officers except for one went back inside.

"I am one of your father's greatest admirers," Guerra said. He wanted the cuffs. He held out his hand expecting her to just lay them on his palm. "A true fan."

"Take a hike, buddy."

Guerra clicked his fingers, and the remaining officer drew his revolver. "Do as you are told," Guerra warned her.

"Hey—I was just kidding." She laid the handcuffs on his palm. "No harm intended, okay?"

"These are supposed to be pick-resistant," he said, testing each lock. "Perhaps you would like to tell me how you opened them."

"I blew on them," she said.

"Did your father teach you how to do this?"

"Yes."

23

"I would like to meet your father," he admitted, slipping the handcuffs into his pocket. "Maybe he'd tell me the secret."

"Don't count on it," Crystal said as the two policemen escorted her through the front doors of the station house.

Chapter 3

London

*L*adies and gentlemen, the Top Hat Club is proud to introduce one of America's finest magicians. Please put your hands together and help me welcome the amazing Hardare."

There was scattered applause, the sound all but drowned out by the drunken couple at a table near the tiny stage. "You bloody fucking bonehead," the woman roared at her husband. "Louise was your first wife. I'm Gloria, remember?"

There was a roar of laughter the precise moment

Hardare stepped on stage. He stood frozen in the spotlight, staring out at the swirling blue haze of smoke that had enveloped the room, unable to make out a single face in the crowd. Seconds passed. He continued to stare. A buzz filled the club like a bad rumor.

"Thank you," he finally stammered into the microphone.

"For what?" the drunken woman roared back at him.

Now the crowd was having fun. Hardare felt a mustache of perspiration forming above his upper lip. *Flopsweat. And I haven't even done my first goddamned trick yet*, he thought, and without waiting for the recorded music to begin, started his act by making a bright red silk scarf appear between his fingers.

Moments later his music clicked on. Stroking the silk several times, he bunched it up and made a flapping white dove appear within its folds. The crowd reacted with a tremendous burst of indifference. Carla, his redheaded assistant, made her appearance, extending her gloved hand so that Hardare could allow the dove to perch there. He did so, and the bird excreted a flowing white liquid on the stage.

There were hoots of laughter. Carla stalked off. Hardare continued the act, trying to remember when in recent memory he had been this bad. Not since high school, vividly remembering the first time he had attempted to do "the birds"—a standard rite of passage for any stage magician—and had failed miserably. He was just as bad tonight, and he was twice as old.

Turning the red carnation in his lapel into a silk handkerchief, he stroked it and made another dove appear. Suddenly a black cane with white tips was twirling in his right hand. He let the bird perch on it, and in a blink of the eye a second dove appeared on the cane, sitting a foot away from the first. He heard real applause this time and felt better. Carla appeared, took the cane, and allowed him to remove a long black scarf from her neck. Tying a knot in its center, he brought the knot up to his teeth, bit into it, and jerking down on the ends of the scarf, caused two doves to appear instantaneously in each hand.

Finally he got a round of applause. Taking a deck of Steamboats from his pocket, he went into his card manipulations. He sprung the cards like an accordian, did his one-hand cuts and shuffles, and snapping the deck into a perfect two-handed fan, caused another dove to appear on the cards. Carla stood beside him holding a top hat and he let the bird perch on its rim.

Fanning the cards in his right hand, he dropped them into the hat, and reaching up, plucked another fan from thin air. He repeated the illusion again and again, then caused single cards to appear in rapid succession, and then in both hands. The audience's reaction was not as strong as he'd expected, and he saw why. A moronic waiter had brought a bottle of champagne to a front table, and the loud-mouthed drunks who had nearly ruined his opening were demanding that the waiter open it. *So much for art*, Hardare thought.

Taking the dove from the hat, Hardare tossed it gently into the air, and a white silk floated down. He caught it, snapped it briskly, and a green silk appeared tied to one end. He untied the silks, snapped the green, and an orange silk appeared in similar fashion. He did this twice more, then bunched the silks together and removed a three-foot-long kicking rabbit from its folds.

27

"Let's hear it for Har-dare!" said the emcee from the wings.

Hardare took a short bow at the precise moment the waiter chose to open the champagne bottle. It exploded a few feet from Hardare's head, and sounded exactly like a rifle discharging. The rabbit, having been raised on a farm, reacted accordingly, and shot a stream of urine into the crowd.

The drunken woman screamed as if she'd been stabbed. Hardare decided to call it a night. With the rabbit drawing blood as it clawed his hands, he made a quick exit into the wings.

The Top Hat's dressing rooms were from the Dark Ages. Small and badly heated, their rustic charm was lost the moment someone tried to change clothes, or pack a suitcase with someone else standing in the room.

"For God's sake, Carla," Hardare argued, holding a handkerchief against his wrist. "I know things haven't been great, but why run out now? The act's going to take off, I can feel it. At least give it a few more weeks."

"No. I'm sick of working in these toilets." She'd changed to jeans and a faded blue cashmere sweater, her scrubbed face making her look eighteen. Hoisting her suitcase off the chair, she backed into him. "Starving I can handle, but not having people laugh at me. If that's what it takes to succeed in this business, then maybe I'd better get out." She started to pack her make-up, then without warning began throwing eyeliner pencils and pancake sponges around the dressing room, a sudden sob escaping her throat. He gently put his arm around her shoulders and pulled her close, remembering how Barbara had cried when something went wrong, or he got hurt. Now he'd found someone else to make miserable.

"I'm really sorry," he whispered, kissing her forehead.

"I know you are. You always are, but you don't change." She dried her eyes on his sleeve. "Look, you'll find another girl, and she'll be pretty, and things will work out fine. They always do."

Their eyes met, and in hers Hardare saw sadness and little else. It was not the ending he had envisioned for them, and he found himself opening the door for her, and following her into the hall.

Several stagehands walked by carrying a backdrop painted like a sunset. Carla gave him a hard, meaningful kiss, being careful not to brush his hand. "How about if I drop by your place tomorrow, pick up my things?"

"The act is getting better," he said, sounding almost defensive.

She touched his cheek. "I just can't stay."

He thought about pleading with her, or making a promise he wouldn't keep, and decided against it. Instead, he simply said, "I guess this is good-bye."

"Please take care of yourself."

"I'll try."

She smiled regretfully, let him ruffle her soft red curls a final time, then walked away, dragging her suitcase through a back door that put her in an alley beside the club, not once looking back.

For a while Hardare sat at the vanity in his dressing room, assessing the tired thirty-six-year-old face in the mirror. For months his agent had accused him of performing by rote, and not breathing any life into the act.

Hardare couldn't argue with him; his performances were mechanical, a dull imitation of his old self. The only excitement in the act seemed to happen when things went wrong. It was hard to believe he'd once been one of the world's highest-paid variety artists, and didn't have to scrounge for jobs.

Time to go home. The thought of the empty town-house depressed him, and he glanced at the snapshot of his daughter taped to the vanity. Maybe he'd been too impulsive in sending her away so suddenly. He missed seeing her hanging around backstage, and wondered if she'd settled into her new life at prep school and promptly forgotten about him. In her last letter she'd sent a report card—the grades were promising—and mentioned a school field trip to Mexico for the holidays. When she got back he'd have to call, surprise her; maybe send a present in the mail. I have to do more things like that, he thought ruefully.

He left the club through a back door. It was pouring rain, the clouds booming with thunder, and he hailed a cab, ducked into the back seat, and gave the driver his address in the West End. His hand hurt from the rabbit's scratches, and Hardare held it in his lap and closed his eyes, trying not to think of his wife, or his daughter, or Carla, or anyone else whose memory tonight would make him immeasurably sad.

Five minutes later he was home. He watched the cab skid away, hurdled a puddle to the curb, then found himself caught in the headlights of a black limousine parked in front of his house. He froze.

A door swung open. "Vincent Hardare."

He could not see through the limo's tinted windows, nor did he recognize the man's deep baritone.

And perhaps whoever was in the car did not really recognize him.

"Nice to meet you," Hardare said pleasantly. "Good night."

"My name is Logan," the voice said. A foot emerged from the limousine. "We'd like to talk to you for a few minutes. In the car, please."

"About what?"

"Your daughter."

The man who spoke was half out of the car and Hardare got a good look at him. Hefty, middle-aged, wearing a Burberry, and, typical of most Americans living here, hatless. No compassion in his face or any true discernible emotion; really nothing at all. "What's this about?" Hardare asked suspiciously just as a cloud seemed to burst above them.

"If you'll just slide in beside me."

"Speak up. I didn't hear you."

"Your daughter—" answered another man, his impassive face appearing in the door "—the one in Acapulco. We *are* talking about the same girl?"

His heart skipped a beat. "Yes. Who are you?"

"My partner and I work with the American embassy," Logan said, opening his wallet to reveal a laminated photo ID with an official-looking stamp. After Hardare had gotten a good look, he said, "Your daughter has been arrested."

Hardare slid into the limousine and onto a cushioned seat opposite the two men. As Logan shut the door, the other man tapped the glass separating them from the uniformed driver. They drove to the end of the block, and took a hard right. Logan started to talk and found himself drowned out.

"Who arrested my girl?" Hardare blurted. "What the hell has she done?" He watched Logan light a Pall Mall while his partner stared absently through dull, thick-lidded eyes. The limousine took another corner without either man saying a word. *I've been around tougher hoods than these two potatoes*, Hardare thought. He began to speak his mind before he remembered that they were talking about Crystal. He decided to shut up and start listening. "Tell me."

"Your daughter was arrested this afternoon in Acapulco for possession of narcotics," Logan said. "Cocaine, to be more specific. She is also being charged with resisting arrest, and assaulting a police officer."

"Give me a break."

"Please . . ."

"My daughter is sixteen years old."

Logan held up his open palm like a cop directing traffic. "I talk, you listen. Otherwise we stop now." He tapped the glass and the limo braked to a halt. When Hardare nodded his head, Logan tapped again and they resumed driving. "Maybe this whole thing is just a big misunderstanding. Or a mistake. Whatever the case, Mexico has a proper judicial system, and the courts will decide. Won't they, Mr. Hardare?"

"What do you want with me?" he said.

"We want you to surrender your passport to us," Logan said. "We don't want you leaving London. And we specifically don't want you traveling to Mexico until this is over."

Hardare stared at Logan and at his silent partner, incredulously. "What are you afraid of—besides one day losing your jobs because of imbecility?"

Logan did not appreciate this, and he jabbed a stiff

forefinger into Hardare's left knee. "We're afraid of the past. Back in 1982 you masterminded the escape of the son of a Texas oil man from a maximum security prison in Colombia, South America. Remember that little caper, Mr. Escape Artist? It put a tremendous strain on diplomatic relations between the United States and Colombia for nearly two years."

"Scott Weiner was being held on a bogus murder rap," Hardare said. "His father came to me when you people wouldn't help him. And all I did was act as a consultant. I never even went to Colombia." He stared into their faces; it was like reasoning with a wall. The limo stopped at a familiar corner, three blocks from his home. He looked into Logan's eyes. "Fuck off," he said defiantly.

"What—?"

"You picked the wrong guy to intimidate," he said, banging his hand against the glass. The limo halted and he threw open the door. "If my daughter is in trouble —and right now, I don't believe a word of this crap— I'm going to help her. And I don't care if it raises the cost of oil imports from Mexico." He jumped onto the curb and stuck his soaking head in the open door. "I can tell you're not the one who runs things, so tell your boss he bombed out on this one. Tell him . . ."

The rain was blowing into the car. Logan tried to step onto the curb but Hardare caught him, pulling the knot in his tie up to his throat, and cutting off his air. "I'm not just some sap who hides in a dark corner when someone makes a loud noise. You hear me, fat boy?"

Logan was losing consciousness, his trembling upper lip betraying the most emotion he'd shown in the past twenty years. Hardare released his strangle hold and shoved him back in the car. "Get out of my neigh-borhood," he roared, and watched the limo sharply grind around a corner and disappear.

His arms were shaking, his clothes now stuck to his skin. He could hear himself breathing. A picture of his daughter sitting in a squalid jail cell tortured his mind. He glanced at his watch and realized it was early enough back in the States to get hold of the headmistress at his daughter's school. She would know what in God's name was going on.

He ran all the way home.

Chapter 4

The American Embassy in London

*E*ight hours later Hardare had not slept, nor changed his clothes. Tipping the cabby a pound note, he bowed his head to the elements and hurried up the brick path of the United States embassy. He had called first thing that morning and spoken to a man named Lyons. He supposed it was a sign of the times that the old Edwardian house resembled Fort Knox, with its barred windows and surveillance cameras perched on the roof, and he found himself walking a little more slowly, hoping his unshaven appearance did not fit the composite of any Libyan terrorists, and that he wouldn't be shot on sight at the front door.

He pressed the doorbell, heard chimes, then an odd clicking. Above the door a camera was focusing on him. He looked into its eye as a gust of wind blew rain down his collar, making him shiver. Taking off his gloves, he rolled them into a ball, then deftly—voila, they were gone. He wiggled his fingers for the camera. "Explain that one to Big Brother," he said, hoping the man inside could hear him.

The front door cracked open. "Yes?" asked a stern-faced woman.

"I'm here to see Richard Lyons. Name's Vincent Hardare. I believe you're expecting me."

She ushered him in, scanning him with a hand-held metal detector. He stood in the foyer, inhaling the special smell of a rich house: waxed mahogany, finely scented furniture polish, thick wool carpets. The downstairs appeared to be empty, which he supposed wasn't unusual, considering the early hour. The woman hung up his wet coat, then escorted him to a two-person elevator like the ones in many older London homes.

"Where did you hide the gloves?" she said as the car rose.

"Can you keep a secret?"

"Of course."

"Good. So can I."

She said "humph" and opened the door to the third floor. He was surprised to find a whirlwind of activity, and she led him past a pool of secretaries typing away silently on word processors to a corner office. Knocking softly, she put her ear to the door as if listening for a heartbeat, then led him in. The office was small but high-ceilinged, and reminded Hardare of an animal's den. On the floor sat books and manuscripts in random piles, while the desk—if it actually existed—lay inches deep in legal papers and letters displaying the colorful embassy seal. Behind the desk stood an anemic preppie, eyeballs popping behind thick pince-nez glasses, his hand extended. "Mr. Hardare, I'm Richard Lyons. Good to meet you."

Over the phone Lyons had sounded big, strapping. In person he looked like a teenage kid going prematurely bald. "Thanks for seeing me so early," Hardare said, almost humbly.

"No problem," Lyons said, indicating the chair across from him. "Please, sit down. Coffee? Or a cup of tea?"

Hardare declined, sitting as the door clicked shut. The English, as Lyons had obviously learned, never offered tea, they offered a cup of tea. He said, "Have you lived in London long?"

"Nearly a year," Lyons said, fishing a yellow pad out of an ominous pile on his desk. He smiled a funny smile which, moments later, Hardare realized was not a smile at all.

"I ran a check on the man who confronted you last night," Lyons went on, "and came up with air. Nobody named Logan has ever been employed by the State Department. Whatever identification he showed you was doctored."

"That doesn't make sense. Why did he demand my passport?"

Lyons shrugged his shoulders. "Maybe he was trying to shake you down, set you up for blackmail. Some of the information he told you was released on a

UPI wire yesterday. So far we don't think it's made any of the newspapers."

Hardare nodded his head absently, still convinced that Logan had wanted something more than money. He looked into Lyons's pale face, and said, "What about my daughter? Did you learn anything from your people in Acapulco?"

"Yes. It isn't good." His eyes returned to the yellow pad. "The officer who arrested your daughter is a top man in the Mexican narcotics division, a Captain Rafael Estavio Guerra. He got a judge to place your daughter in protective custody. That means we can't see her, or get her version of what happened, until their investigation is completed and she's released."

"Investigation of what?"

"Your daughter was arrested for narcotics possession. I suppose they want to know who sold it to her, and whether or not she was planning to smuggle it back into the States."

"For Christ's sake, she's in the eleventh grade. And she's traveled around the world enough to know you don't go buying pot from strangers."

"She was arrested with three kilos of uncut cocaine in her possession and a few thousand dollars cash. Maybe her friends put her up to it, passed the hat around at school and then drew straws to see who would make the score once they made it to Acapulco. If that wasn't the case . . . " He let the thought drift.

"What are you trying to do—convince me that she's guilty? This is my child, mister."

"I'm not trying to convince you of anything, just make you aware of the facts." Lyons came around the desk, picked up a manila folder, and displayed two badly reproduced eight-by-ten black and white glossies. "Do you recognize this handbag?"

Hardare squinted, barely making out the Gucci emblem on the metal snap. Last Christmas he'd wasted the better part of two days canvassing Harrod's and the other department store boutiques looking for that bag. "Yes."

"This is what Captain Guerra and his men found inside it." He put the second photograph inches from Hardare's disbelieving eyes. "A bag of snow and more cash than I've ever held at one time in my entire life. That's reason enough for them to hold her."

Hardare looked down at the floor and took a deep breath. After a minute's pause he said, "What are we supposed to do now?"

Lyons said, "Excuse me?"

"To get her out of jail. What kind of help are your people prepared to give me?"

Lyons frowned. He removed his outdated glasses and wiped them with an embroidered handkerchief, refolded it carefully so the monogram was showing, and put it back in his breast pocket, still saying nothing. For an awkward moment they traded stares, until Hardare realized that this was his answer. He stared at the sallow official in disbelief; the blood drained from his head.

Down on the street the sounds of people going to work were a cacophony of muffled chords. Hardare's eyes drifted across the confusion on the desk and fell on a framed portrait of Lyons with his family at the beach. He picked it up, feeling an odd comfort in their tan and happy faces. "You have a wife, two little girls. Families are important; they're the glue that keeps our lives together. Two years ago I lost my wife in a car accident. Crystal is all I have left. A few months ago I sent her away to boarding school, and I still miss her every day. Having her locked up in jail is driving me out of my mind."

"It isn't an easy thing to accept," Lyons said.

"I'm not accepting it," he replied, growing livid. "She's not a criminal, and I won't allow her to be treated like one. Nor should you."

"Then you're making it hard on yourself. Do you mind?" He seemed uncomfortable with Hardare holding the portrait, and as he tried to take it back, Hardare gripped the frame with both hands. Lyons pulled forcefully, and they tugged back and forth, like two stubborn dogs with a bone. The color rose in Lyons's cheeks. "Let it go, God damn it!"

Finally Hardare released the frame and left several smudge marks on the glass over the family's smiling faces. Lyons raised his arm as if to hit him; instead he took out his handkerchief again. "That was uncalled for," he said, carefully wiping the frame clean.

"We get protective when it comes to our families."

"Look, I empathize with you, and I want to help—"

"You do?" Hardare stood, towering over him. "Then why are you sticking a big bureaucratic tit in my mouth? Just tell me how to get my girl out of Mexico. Do I bribe a judge, or this clown Guerra? That's how their legal system works, isn't it? Grease a few palms and all is forgiven. It's a great little scam, and I'm willing to play along. Just tell me how much, and I'll pay it, no questions asked."

Lyons stared into his face, studying his eyes. "Let's take a walk, get some breakfast." He went to the door, removing a beige London Fog from a hook. "I know what you want: I just don't want to discuss it here."

A deep breath escaped Hardare's lungs. He'd finally broken through. He followed Lyons out the door.

The Thames Inn was the English equivalent of a greasy spoon, located a few blocks from the embassy. The waitress on duty seated them in a booth by the window, took their orders, then brought them two cups of bitter coffee and a plastic basket of sourdough rolls baked a day or two before.

"If your daughter isn't released soon," Lyons said, buttering a roll, "a meeting will be arranged in Washington with officials from the Mexican consulate." He bit into the roll, but after several vigorous chews, seemed to lose his appetite. "We can file an official protest, make it clear that her jailing can seriously damage our relations with Mexico. That will make them jump. Your lawyers can then follow up."

Their waitress brought two plates of questionable-looking food. Lyons plunged a fork into a mound of runny scrambled eggs while Hardare considered leaving then and there, and looking elsewhere for help. There were hundreds of hapless American kids being held in foreign prisons. Why should anyone in Washington care about Crystal, especially if the Scott Weiner incident was still raising hackles? "What will your people in Washington do," he said, "refuse to attend cocktail parties sponsored by the Mexican government?"

Wiping his chin, Lyons said, "Try to control your

41

temper. We have to hope for the best. There aren't many other alternatives right now."

"That's not true."

"Really?" Lyons raised his fork to his mouth. "I'd be interested in hearing what they are."

"I could fly to Acapulco this afternoon, break into their jail, and free her myself."

Lyons's fork hit the plate with a jarring clang. Two tables over a woman with peroxide hair lifted her eyes from her racy Fleet Street tabloid. Hardare fielded her questioning stare, and when she did not look away, blew a kiss. Insulted, she lowered her gaze, and became quickly absorbed with the latest scandals.

"Come on," Lyons said. "You're joking."

"Not at all. I'd do it tomorrow."

The diplomat's boyish face wrinkled with genuine concern. "Look, breaking into prisons is strictly Hollywood stuff. It doesn't happen in the real world. People foolish enough to try usually get killed."

"Let me tell you something," Hardare said. "There isn't a prison in the world that can't be broken into."

"You're serious, aren't you." Lyons pushed his plate forward, no longer hungry. "Tell me something. How many prisons have you broken into?"

"I haven't broken into any," Hardare admitted, "but I've broken out of over thirty. All maximum security."

"*What?* You're putting me on."

"My uncle was Harry Houdini," Hardare said icily. "I'm a professional magician and escape artist. Opening locked doors is one of my specialties."

"I thought your name was familiar." Lyons rubbed his chin, straining his memory. "I saw you on the tube a few times. Tell me something. The time you jumped out of the plane with your arms handcuffed behind you. Were those cuffs real?"

"Regulation Smith and Wessons."

"Jesus." He shook his head. "What if you hadn't opened them in time?"

"Human pancake."

Lyons laughed faintly. "Why break out of prisons?"

"For the publicity. Houdini's first prison escape was in Chicago in 1898. The Chicago newspapers talked about it for weeks. Houdini taught my father his secrets, and my father passed them on to me. Prison breaks make good box office."

"But that's a staged act," Lyons argued. "Real prisons are filled with armed guards and attack dogs. How would you protect yourself?"

"First of all, she's not in a prison," Hardare reminded him. "She's in a downtown city jail. The security wouldn't be nearly as rigid. I'd be in and out before they knew it. All I would need is a person who knows his firearms to back me up."

"*You mean a mercenary?*" Lyons reached for his wallet to pay for the uneaten food. "Let me make sure I'm hearing you correctly. You're actually considering hiring someone to break into the Acapulco city jail to help free your daughter?"

"If it's necessary," Hardare said, vaguely recalling the crusty techo jock that had been hired to stage Scott Weiner's escape.

Lyons was thinking too. Without another word Lyons abandoned his food, put a few pounds on the table, and walked outside. Hardare followed him into the continuing rain, and waited on the corner while

Lyons opened his retractable umbrella with a small flourish.

"Mr. Hardare, please be patient." They crossed the street and Hardare turned his collar up to the cold. "Give me a little time to see what I can do on my end. If Crystal isn't freed soon, we'll explore the possibilities of what you just mentioned. But for God's sake, don't do anything without first contacting me. Being an escape artist doesn't make you superman. I once read that the reason Houdini died was because he let some college kid hit him in the stomach to demonstrate his muscle control. He thought he could take it, but the kid ruptured his appendix, and it killed him. Now take a look at yourself. You think you can rescue Crystal just by clicking your fingers. It isn't that easy. You might get killed, and that will put Crystal in worse shape than she's in right now."

They had reached the embassy, and Hardare said, "You know someone, don't you? A soldier for hire."

"Yes, I do," Lyons said quietly.

"Will you tell me his name?"

For a long moment Lyons stared at Hardare. Finally, he said, "If it comes down to that, yes."

"Thank you."

They shook hands and Lyons said, "I'll call you as soon as I hear anything from my people in Mexico. Now go home and get some sleep. You look like hell."

And up until an hour ago, had felt like it. He watched Lyons walk away in the pouring rain, his spirits uplifted.

* * *

To his dismay, Lyons returned to his borrowed office to find Dorsey sitting behind his desk, puffing amiably on a hand-rolled Honduran cigar he'd lifted from the humidor. "What are you doing in here?" Lyons said, retiring his umbrella to a brass pail in the corner. "Reading the garbage?"

"Actually I was admiring your work." Dorsey held up his family photograph as a smoke-ring gravitated above him, drifted on invisible currents across the room, and dispersed against a bookcase like a cloud hitting a mountainside. "This is a nice touch. Makes me really believe this is your office. By the way, this your real wife and kids?"

"Yes, they're my wife and kids," Lyons said, unbuttoning his jacket. "I didn't see anywhere in the budget for fake ones. Something wrong with that?"

"You let him see your family. If he ever turns against us, you've given him three good targets."

"That portrait was taken five years ago," Lyons said defensively. "Mary's changed her hair color, and both my girls have grown."

Dorsey puffed his stolen cigar, listening but not listening. He held up that morning's edition of *The New York Times*. "You brought your newspaper, another nice touch. Except it has an address label. Now he knows where you live, and what your family looks like."

"Maybe he didn't see it."

"Assume that he did."

Dorsey's logic exasperated him. "Why?" Lyons asked.

"Because if you don't, one morning your wife and kids will get in the car, and your wife will start the

45

ignition, and you won't have any wife and kids anymore." He flicked an ash into the wastebasket. "Didn't
they teach you any precautionary measures at Langley?"

"If our London staff wasn't so goddamned lean,
I'd put you on the street." Lyons slapped his hand on
the desk, sending papers to the floor. Two years running
the London operation and Dorsey still treated him like
a bumbling Eagle Scout. Lyons wanted to fire his ass
for insubordination—had tried his first week on the
job—and learned what the consequences would be.
Washington would send a replacement without any foreign experience; a rookie. On second thought he had
shredded the letter requesting Dorsey's dismissal, and
done the best he could to work with him.

"I'm just trying to cover your ass," Dorsey said,
slapped by the threat. "Your background isn't in undercover, and I don't want to see you hurt. You look
out for me, I look out for you. That's how the game is
played."

"Apology accepted."

Suddenly the office door opened. It was Logan.

"Hell of a job, Rich. Very convincing." He was out
of breath from taking the stairs, his latest effort to trim
his bulging waistline. Ripping off his baggy raincoat, he
gripped Lyons enthusiastically on the shoulder. "You
had him eating out of your hand. I was impressed."

Lyons stared at him in bewilderment. "Come
again?"

"The way you maneuvered Hardare over breakfast.
Told him just enough to get him worked up. He's
hooked."

"You were there? Where?"

"You said you might take him out to eat, so I

guessed the Thames. I was sitting in a booth behind you, reading a paper."

Of the London field agents, Logan was everyone's best man. To look at, he wasn't much; pudgy, stoop-shouldered, his balding hair formed what Lyons's two girls called a toilet bowl head, while his clothes regularly included old faded suits and stained ties, the styles dating back to when everyone wore Brooks Brothers. Hidden behind the confusion was a razor-sharp mind and street smarts so brilliant that it made you wonder if the outer layer was just a clever disguise.

From his pocket Logan took a teletype printout. Lyons did not take it from him, preferring to hear Logan's translation. "Good news or bad?"

"Our agents in Acapulco located the jail," Logan said. "Security looks pretty standard. We can get some of our people in there, but they'll have to be heavily armed."

"And risk shooting it out with the police?" Lyons said, knowing how the men above him thought. "You're talking about an international incident now, and that's definitely out of the question, no matter how much Maria Alvarez knows."

Lyons went to the window, staring down at cars on the treacherously slick macadam, looking for a solitary figure and thinking he saw him blocks away, walking with resolution and purpose through the cold penetrating rain. "What we need is a phantom. Someone who can open locks silently. A real life escape artist." He grew silent, watching the tiny figure disappear. "Vincent Hardare is ready made. But there is one problem."

"What is that?" Logan said, sharing the view.

"He's hotheaded. He doesn't think he needs us. I have to convince him otherwise." Lyons retrieved the file on Crystal from the desk. "Keep an eye on him. If he tries to leave England before we're ready, I want him stopped."

Logan glanced at Dorsey. "We'll make sure he doesn't go anywhere," he said.

Instead of going home, Hardare bought an umbrella and took a walk. It was one of those great iron mornings in London, the sky blanketed by black clouds and a thousand chimneys coughing up soot and waste. The weather matched his mood, and for an hour he walked the narrow streets aimlessly, his thoughts warped in the past. Turning a corner, he saw the majestic spire of St. Paul's cathedral, and realized he was heading due east, and into one of the city's most impoverished districts.

It was not his favorite section of London. With each passing block the scenery faded and the magnificent facades of banks and office buildings gave way to deteriorating storefronts and rows of low-end apartments. Young girls stood in doorways, silently beckoning him, and he saw packs of roaming youths with spiked hairdos and outlandish punk rocker clothes. They looked like visitors from outer space, and as he walked among them, catching an occasional stare or hard look, he realized he was the alien. He was from fashionable West End; and despite his problems, he did have money, and a place to live, and a decent line of work. His dilemmas were minor compared to their empty lives, and he began to think a little more clearly about his situation.

At the corner a milk truck splashed his shoes. Inside a street stall a toothless hag was selling flowers. She stuck a wilted bouquet in his face and hawked, "Twopence for the bunch. Take them home to the one you love. Twopence."

"No, thanks," he said, flipping her a coin. He started to cross, and in the middle of the street heard an eruption of angry voices. Down on the corner two red-faced bobbies were running in a wino, who in an act of self-preservation had latched onto a parked car door. He howled mournfully, like a dog baying at the full moon. Hardare wondered why, in a country where it was legal to buy heroin and methadone it could also be a crime to drown your sorrows.

"You bloody sods," the wino bellowed as the bobbies pried his arms free, and dragged him kicking and screaming away. "I was just sleeping it off—stop kicking me, you thick-headed bastard."

A delivery truck's horn sent Hardare leaping for the curb. When he glanced up the street again, the wino was gone, vanished behind the swinging glass doors of the station house. What an old fort, he thought, staring from beneath his dripping umbrella. The station house was bleached gray, built of stone and mortar in a turn-of-the-century style. He tried to envision the jail in Acapulco, and thought of all the things that could go wrong during a break-in. Was he a lunatic to believe he could singlehandedly break in and out of a place like this?

He gave it a minute's thought. Lyons was right; it was a hell of a lot more difficult than he'd made it sound. Maybe in frustration he'd made a claim he couldn't live up to. He took a deep breath. Only one sure way to find out.

He began walking down the puddled sidewalk.

Slowly at first, taking short steps, letting himself build momentum. Then a little more briskly until he reached the station house steps. He ran up the short flight and through the swinging doors, his shoes skidding on the shiny marble floor. Behind the front desk a pot-bellied sergeant was drawing circles on a newspaper. His nameplate identified him as Sergeant R. Foley.

"That was quite an entrance," Foley said.

"I used to be with the Ice Capades."

The policeman didn't get the joke. "Need some help?"

"Yes . . . well, no. This might sound strange."

"Try me."

"I'd like to be locked up in your jail."

"You don't say." Foley scrutinized him, and Hardare noticed the man's bulbous nose and puffy red complexion. A saloon tan. "Care to talk about it?" Foley said.

"Talk about what?"

"Whatever's bothering you. Maybe you beat the wife, or robbed the corner store. You must have done something wrong."

"No . . . "

Foley stared at the bandage on his wrist. "Get shot?"

"Oh, no—just a scratch."

Foley squinted at him. "Mister, I haven't got time for games. Have you, or haven't you broken any laws?"

He wasn't giving him a chance. "No, but—"

"Positive?"

"Yes, but—"

"Afraid I can't help you," said the sergeant. "This is a police station, not a bleeding hotel. We have rules for keeping people in, and rules for keeping people out. If we didn't, every poor bloke in London would be dropping in for a hot meal and a bed. Now if you'll excuse me, I have work to do." Picking up his pencil, Foley went back to circling entries in that day's racing form. Without looking up he said, "Good morning."

Hardare didn't move. He tried to explain but Foley rustled his paper loudly, all but drowning him out. Damn. Picking up the coffee on the desk, Hardare held it above the newspaper, said, "I'm sorry about this." and poured.

Foley sprang up with a roar. He moved with speed uncharacteristic for a man his size, and coming around the desk, this incongruity caught up with him. His foot caught the desk leg and he fell, hitting the marble floor with an anguished cry. Hardare rushed to his side, helping him to stand.

"That's it, put your weight against me."

"Twisted my bleeding ankle. Cripes, that hurts!" They did a three-legged walk around the lobby, and Foley said, "Know something, Yank? I'm going to lock you up for that."

"That was the idea," Hardare said.

"Very funny." The policeman twisted Hardare's arm behind him and took a ring of keys from his pocket. "You want me to treat you like a criminal? Fine. Let's go. I'll book you when I feel like doing it."

The cellblock was in the back. On the way Foley unlocked two steel doors, and Hardare memorized the makes of the keys Foley used. Passing through the property room, Foley picked up a number of handcuffs lying on a desk, and rustled them loudly as he brusquely pushed Hardare ahead.

The actual cellblock was small, with two facing rows of five cells. The handful of prisoners there—mostly drunks and dispirited bums—waved or called "Good morning." As Hardare waved back, Foley opened an empty cell and pushed him inside.

"Stand against the wall," Foley said, following him into the cell. The sergeant had grabbed four pairs of cuffs, and he made Hardare remove his raincoat and roll back his shirt sleeves, then tightly snapped all four pairs of cuffs around Hardare's wrists and up his forearms.

Hardare kept his biceps flexed and watched intently. Perhaps it was an economy measure, but in England only five makes of cuffs were used by the police. These cuffs had a single ratchet on each side, and rarely gave the magician trouble. To open them, he would use a five-inch steel lockpick that he kept stuck behind his belt, where it blended invisibly with the dark leather.

The other prisoners were now standing by their cell doors, watching the show. When Foley was done he said, "That should hold you for a little while."

"Maybe," Hardare said.

One of the prisoners laughed. With an angry look, the sergeant reached into his back pocket and removed a pair of plastic riot cuffs. "Know what these are?" he said indignantly. "We use them on those I.R.A. bastards. They don't come with a key. We have to cut them off. Think you'd like to try them on, Yank?"

"Why not?" Hardare said. Pressing his wrists together, he let Foley put the cuffs above the others on the thickest part of his forearms. The plastic dug into his flesh, and Hardare said, "You're cutting off the circulation."

"Too bad," Foley replied, tightening them even more. Then he backed out of the cell and banged the barred door shut. "Have a nice nap. I'll be back in a few hours."

"Don't forget to lock the doors behind you," Hardare called after him.

The cellblock door slammed. "That Foley can be a mean cuss," one of the prisoners told him.

"He certainly can," Hardare agreed, plucking the lockpick from behind his belt. He jammed it into the bottom pair of cuffs, and in seconds had them opened. He jiggled his arms and sent the opened pair flying into the bars.

"Do that again!" shouted a prisoner.

"Sure." Using muscle control, Hardare moved the four remaining pairs down his forearms. Then he jammed the lockpick in, his fingers a blur. When he had performed this routine on stage years ago, he had been accompanied by music played pizzicatto on the violin, the plucking chords in tempo with his movements. He jiggled his arms rhythmically, and sent the second pair of cuffs flying.

No one in the world did it faster; no one. Years ago, the International Brotherhood of Magicians had held a contest pitting five rival escape artists, and Hardare had escaped minutes ahead of one of his peers, and then stood talking with reporters while his rivals had wrestled with their stubborn handcuffs and leg irons.

Within moments the third and fourth pairs of handcuffs were airborne. The prisoners were watching his progress with great enthusiasm, and when he casually slipped the plastic riot cuffs off by dislocating his wrists, they burst into applause.

"Do another trick," several urged him. "Do another."

"I will," he promised, and opened the cell door.

Goddamn rude pushy Americans!

Hobbling to his desk, Foley slammed his body into his chair. Here it was, not ten in the morning and his entire day was ruined. His ankle was throbbing, the *Globe* was soaked, his coffee gone. For a minute he toyed with the idea of taking the Yank into a back room and giving him a swift taste of English justice.

He was lost in fantasies of revenge when the front door opened, and a dripping wet man entered the station house. Foley stared, nearly falling off his chair.

"You!"

"Sorry for all the trouble," Hardare said, taking a folded paper from beneath his arm. "*The Globe* was sold out, so I bought you a copy of *The Examiner*."

Foley's words came slowly. "This is some kind of trick. You're not the bloke I locked up."

"Of course I am." Hardare said. "Same raincoat, same wet head of hair. Don't I look the same?"

No, Foley thought, he doesn't; the physical resemblance was there, but this fellow was more relaxed than the man he'd jailed. "You're not him. You're a twin."

"My folks should have been so lucky. If you don't mind." He retrieved his umbrella from beside the desk. "Thanks again."

"For what?"

54

"Locking me up. I really appreciate it."

Then he was out the door. Was this on the level? Maybe someone was playing a practical joke on him, like the blokes on the telly. Jumping up, he knocked over his chair, and hobbling on his bad leg, fumbled with the keys as he unlocked the two steel doors and went into the cellblock.

Only to discover every single cell empty! Except for one.

The cell he had locked the Yank in. But the Yank was gone. In his place in that cell were all the other inmates. They were playing cards with a weathered deck, and refused to acknowledge him as he leaned against the bars.

"Where's the flipping American?" Foley asked them.

The bum dealing cards glanced up. "Who?"

"The bloke in the fancy raincoat. Where is he?"

The bum looked to the others, and they grinned at their private joke. "I guess you could say he escaped."

"But how?" Foley clutched the bars to their communal cell and saw the pile of handcuffs on the floor. "How did he do it?"

A white-haired drunk whispered to the dealer. "What's your friend saying?" Foley demanded.

"Charlie thinks he knows how he escaped," the bum said.

Foley leaned forward anxiously. "Will you tell me?"

"Sure. Charlie thinks he used mirrors."

Chapter 5

Santa Maria

*T*hey drove continuously through the desert for eight hours.

Riding shotgun in the lead van, Guerra anxiously puffed on a cigarette while staring into his mirror. It had been an exhausting afternoon. The first tail had appeared ten miles outside of Acapulco, a black Ford Thunderbird. It followed them for twenty minutes, then turned off. Five hours and three hundred miles later, his driver had spotted a low-flying Cessna on Highway 87. It had stayed overhead a good five minutes. The third tail had materialized a few minutes ago in the form of a white Toyota pick-up, its shiny bumpers easy to see in the bright sunlight.

Guerra laughed bitterly. It was not a funny situation, yet he still found it amusing that the DEA was better equipped and trained than his own police force. Newer cars, expensive planes, sophisticated communications equipment, more dedicated people, and the irony was they were now in a foreign country. *My country.* Up ahead he could faintly see a cluster of buildings; he judged they were fifteen minutes from their final destination. "Pull over," he told the driver.

They parked on the highway's shoulder, the second van with their prisoners directly behind. Guerra watched his mirror: the white pick-up also pulled over. Now we're on equal terms, he thought, crushing out his cigarette. He got out with his driver, who was cradling a high-powered rifle.

Sensing trouble, the two policemen in the second van joined them, both armed with shotguns. Guerra made them assemble on the side of the road. He stared into their dull, expressionless faces and for a long moment struggled with his anger.

"You are idiots." Guerra checked himself: what was the point in reprimanding them? Instead of learning from their mistakes, they would only turn bitter. He pointed down the highway. "Did any of you notice we were being followed?"

They gave him slack-jawed stares. Stepping out of line, his driver raised his rifle, squinting through the telescopic sight. He dejectedly lowered his gun. "Too far," he mumbled.

Guerra touched his arm. "If the pick-up drives towards us, shoot it off the road." To the other driver he said, "Let's teach these people a lesson. Get the whores out of your van."

The driver unlocked the van and let out a sharp bark. From out of the back crawled four women prisoners, their ankles and wrists manacled together by an intricate device called a Siberian chain. The van was not air-conditioned, and the women—faces ghostly pale, eyes sallow, hair stringy and lifeless—looked like death warmed over. They stood on the burning asphalt, and when a barefoot prostitute complained that her toes were burning, the driver said, "This will take your mind off it," and cuffed her in the head.

"It would have been so easy to have avoided all of this," Guerra said to Maria Alvarez. Someone had given her a bad beating at the jail, and her high cheekbones were doughy and discolored. She looked vulnerable without her paint and fancy clothes. Grasping her by the hair, he pulled her head back so she was staring into the sun. To his driver he said, "What are the men in the pick-up doing?"

"Watching us," he replied, peering through his gun sight. "With binoculars. One of them is talking into a radio."

"Good." To the other driver he said, "Unlock this one, and the girl."

The driver released Maria and Crystal, then handcuffed both women behind their backs, and made them kneel in the dirt. Drawing his revolver, Guerra placed it against Maria's temple, stiffening his arm as if to shoot her.

He paused, anxious to see how the men in the pick-up reacted. Maybe they thought he was bluffing. If so, they were also idiots. Executions often occurred in the deserts outside Mexico City, and were blamed on the infamous Death Squads, who ritualistically shot their victims in the head and dumped them beside the highway in a burning heap. The newspapers claimed the squads were rival gangs bumping each other off. Another popular theory was that vigilante policeman rid their jails of habitual offenders this way. Guerra, who had spent little time in this area, didn't know, and didn't care. He only hoped the men in the pick-up read the newspapers.

Seconds passed. Frustrated, he made a show of cocking his revolver. He saw Maria's tears plop against the asphalt, heard Crystal praying to herself. "What are they doing?" he asked his driver.

"Nothing. Watching us."

Stalling, like him. Damn them. One of these women was a DEA agent, and he wanted the men in the pick-up to tell him which one she was.

First he had thought it was Crystal. The check he had run through the computers at their modernized facility in Mexico City had turned up nothing about her, but revealed a great deal about her energetic father. Years ago Vincent Hardare had helped the heir to a Texas oil fortune escape from a maximum security prison in South America, and although the incident had drawn international criticism, and several protests at the United Nations, Hardare had never been arrested. It only made sense if he was working as an undercover agent. He was internationally known, a status that would place him above suspicion almost anywhere he traveled. And his props—what an ideal place to hide guns, or secret communication equipment. They were a team, Guerra had decided; father and daughter working together, moving freely from one country to another, the perfect veils for espionage work.

Except it was all speculation. Everything he knew, he really didn't know. And she was still just a teenager; still chewing Wrigley's Spearmint, driving with a temporary permit, probably still a virgin. On the surface Maria Alvarez was a more likely candidate. He knew she was a courier. But was she more than that? He had shifted his probe. Using her driver's license and social identification number, he'd effortlessly dug into her past.

Born in a *barrio* of Acapulco, she came from a family of eight children, with a father who worked as a tailor. Nowhere did he find mention of her mother, a fact that made him assume the woman had died years ago, and that her files had been routinely destroyed. Maria's father was indigent but hard-working, and had instilled his ethics in his children. Each had graduated high school, and four, including Maria, had earned scholarships to college or received vocational training.

After college Maria had gone to Mexico City, become an editor at *Carta Editorial de Mexico*, which published Mexican *Vogue*, then quit after four years. No work history was available on the computers after that. On a hunch he had telephoned her past employers, spoken to the head of personnel. According to her, Maria was an *enfant terrible*; her articles on women's liberation had drawn sackfuls of hate mail, and boosted newsstand sales fifteen percent. Why had she left? Her brother Manuel had been murdered in a drug deal gone sour and Maria, who had raised him, took it very hard. Yes, the magazine had tried to hire her back. No, no one knew where she'd gone, or what she was doing.

Guerra had found a fat file on Manuel. It seemed that among Mr. Alvarez's eight children there had been one black sheep. Manuel had been arrested a dozen times for peddling coke, and one day was found lying outside his father's house in broad daylight with his throat slit. The killing had sounded vaguely familiar to Guerra, and he had wondered if he had ordered it himself. It was hard to remember; he had killed so many dealers who had threatened to expose him, he had started forgetting names.

But that wasn't important. What was important was how Manuel's murder had affected Maria. Had she known he was dealing dope, and decided to seek revenge by becoming a DEA agent? If that was true, he could probably assume she was directly after *him*, and if given the chance would kill him. Again, he was speculating. Maybe she was, as she vehemently claimed, just acting as a courier. Guerra couldn't be sure.

He fired his revolver into the dirt. Shuddering, Maria fell face first onto the asphalt. To his driver he said, "Anything?"

"No, sir."

He placed his revolver against Crystal's skull. What were the men in the pick-up thinking? It was hard to say, yet he felt certain that if they thought one of their own was about to be "retired," they'd try to prevent it.

The wind picked up, sweeping dust across the deserted highway. Suddenly the driver let out a short cry and held his rifle as if to fire. Guerra squinted at the pick-up; was it moving toward them, or had the swirling wind fooled his driver into thinking he saw movement, when there was none?

A cloud of white sand swirled around the pick-up.

"Don't shoot," he ordered, taking the rifle and peering through the telescopic sight. Glimpses of the pick-up appeared in the swirling sand, then just as quickly vanished. At one moment he thought the pick-up was stationary, the next that it was driving straight toward them.

What if the men in the pick-up had called for a back-up? He didn't believe in taking chances, and began firing. Two of his men joined in, and the thunder of their gunfire reverberated across the desert. Just as suddenly as it had picked up, the wind settled, and they all stopped firing at once. Guerra stood in the middle of the highway, his men flanking him, speechless.

The pick-up truck had disappeared. Gone like a mirage, or a figment of their collective imaginations. Guerra did not like it; it was the kind of stunt he expected someone like Crystal's father to pull. "Put them in the van," he commanded, then noticed Crystal lying unconscious beside Maria. He nudged her with his heel. When she didn't move, he knelt beside her, and lifted her eyelid with the tip of his thumb.

When Crystal awoke, she was lying on a springy cot in a concrete prison cell. She blinked several times, and for a few unbearable moments could not move. Dirty Levis and soiled women's underwear were strewn across the cell, reminding her of laundry day back at school.

On the wall beside her cot, faded fashion magazines and yellowing paperbacks lined shelves made from fruit crates. Above the crates flashy postcards were Scotch-taped to the wall, and she saw pictures: Disney World, Knott's Berry Farm, Six Flags Over Texas, and one of her favorite places, Windows on the World in New York. The bright scenes made her terribly homesick, and she sat bolt upright with a dull aching pain in her stomach.

She burst out crying, the tears running freely down her face. What the hell was happening to her, and why, and what had she done to deserve this? And where was her father, and the chaperones from the trip, and her friends from school? Didn't they realize what a horrible nightmare she was in, or didn't they care? Her classmates were probably back at Rosemary Hall, safe in their dorm rooms. Sobs choked her throat, making it difficult for her to breathe. She was afraid to try and guess what lay ahead.

She walked around the cell on rubbery legs. There was a tiny window, and she stared down at a pounded dirt courtyard, and beyond that to two barbed wire fences that looked twenty feet high. In each corner of the yard stood guard towers with turreted machine guns aiming down at the heads of gray-shirted inmates passing below. Her father often called prisons tombs, and now she understood why. This place was huge, as big as her school and certainly with as many people, and here she was locked in the center of it, like a dumb gerbil in a cage in a pet shop in a gigantic department store.

She tested the cell door; it was locked solid. The enameled bars were worn smooth where inmates instinctively held them at chest height. She could see five cells in the cellblock, and she sniffed the heavy odor of a strong disinfectant. From the hall she heard footsteps, and watched a young guard enter the block, glancing casually into each cell. He made a mark in a notebook and started to leave.

"Please," Crystal implored, "don't go. Look, do you speak any English?"

"Depends who I'm speaking to," he replied without a hint of accent. He was young, and bore the distinction of not having a Burt Reynolds mustache. He stuck his smooth almond-colored face inches from the bars. "Make it fast. I'm on duty."

She gazed at him pleadingly. "Look, I'm not a criminal. I haven't broken any laws." Silence. She bit her lip. "You have to believe me. I'm telling the truth."

"Of course you are," he insisted.

"You believe me?"

The guard nodded. "Your problem is a universal one. Every inmate in Santa Maria is innocent. Not one of you has committed a crime. You were all falsely arrested and wrongfully convicted. The real criminals are running the country, and doing it badly, I might add. The world is falling apart." He tried to touch her, to caress her left breast, and Crystal jumped back. Grinning wickedly, he stuck his pink tongue between the bars.

"See you later, alligator," he sang, making an obscene clicking sound. Then he left.

"Up yours," she called after him as the door was shut.

"Hey, you."

"Huh?"

"Over here."

The woman's voice came out of nowhere. Drying her eyes, Crystal put her face to the bars. In the cell cater-corner to hers stood Maria Alvarez in a gray work shirt and a pair of white cotton panties. They had been kept on different floors in the jailhouse in Acapulco, and on the bus hadn't talked for fear of being beaten. A dozen questions jumped to Crystal's mind, yet she hesitated before saying a word; for whatever reason, Maria was responsible for her being here; trusting her might only make things worse, if that was possible.

"What's up?" she asked, her chest tightening.

"How are you feeling? You hit the pavement very hard." Maria took a charred cigarette stub out of her breast pocket and lit up. Her hair was shiny clean and parted in the center, and the puffiness had left her face and been replaced with a dark, radiant glow. "You were talking in your sleep, yelling for your dad. I tried to wake you. Sounded like a bad nightmare."

Crystal clenched the bars and her nightmare came back to her. She'd been at the bottom of a deep well, the water gushing around her, inches from her chin. Her father had lowered himself on a rope and she had jumped up, trying to grab his outstretched hand. She missed, tried again, missed, screamed, looked into his face, saw him crying. That's when she woke up. "What time is it?"

"Almost four. You've been out a while. A doctor gave you a shot when we arrived." Maria exhaled a billowing volume of smoke that created a filmy haze in the cellblock. Outside the sun had slipped behind the clouds, and the effect was like the lights going down in a theater. "This is Santa Maria Acatila Penitentiary, about fifty miles northwest of Mexico City, in case you're interested." She felt Crystal's stare and looked at the floor. "Look, I'm sorry I got you involved in this . . ."

"Why did you?"

"It was an accident," She crushed the butt against a bar, then pocketed it. "Guerra's men saw you on the balcony, thought we were working together."

"Why didn't you tell them the truth?"

"I tried to."

"Bullshit." Then, "You didn't try hard enough."

"I was drowning," Maria said sharply. "Any idea what that's like? You pull down whoever's near you. I'm sorry."

"What's Guerra going to do. Kill us?"

Maria hesitated, sensing that this girl had the uncanny ability to know precisely when she was telling the truth, and when she was not. Despite her age, Crystal spoke with an adult's voice, and generally said what was on her mind. Guerra had convinced himself she was an agent, and now Maria knew why.

"I don't think so," she said, listening to footsteps in the hall. "He wouldn't have brought us here for that. We're worth more to him alive than in graves."

"How come?"

"He'll offer us as a trade. That's why he's gone to such elaborate measures to be sure no one can rescue us."

"You mean we're hostages."

"Very good." She smothered a tired yawn. "I must lie down. I haven't slept much in the past two days."

Crystal felt an emptiness swell in her chest. "How long will he keep us here? A few weeks, a month?"

"As long as he wants." Maria said, her voice growing thin. "A month, maybe a year."

Crystal watched Maria lie down on a cot. A whole year? She hadn't spent that much time in one place since the eighth grade, back when her mom was alive and her father was still a headliner and working a year at a time in the better hotels in Las Vegas and Lake Tahoe. In a year she'd be almost eighteen and her friends at school would have graduated. In a year she'd be able to get an adult driver's license and stop being treated like a child.

She stared at the cell's grimy walls. Normally she could stare at a wall and imagine a landscape with lush green trees and jagged rivers and snowcapped mountains where clouds should be; her imagination's vision of *the* perfect place. But the wall in her cell wasn't a screen, or a mirror to her thoughts. It was cold, thick, rough-edged concrete. What would a year here be like, shut away from the real world?

She continued staring, and soon the cell became like a *picture* of a cell, though more murky, and then it sank away and became tiny, as though she was looking at it through the wrong end of a telescope. She shut her eyes, hoping the distorted picture would go away, but the tiny cell stayed right there, as if permanently etched in her thoughts.

An hour later Crystal forced herself to get up. Her mind had filled with depressing memories, and she kept seeing her mother calling out to her moments before she died. But that was stupid; her mother had been unconscious, and hadn't spoken a word.

She paced the cell, counting her footsteps. That was odd; same size as her dorm room, without the closet. It would have been nice to pretend the rooms were the same, and that she could simply daydream the hours away. But she couldn't walk down the hall to buy a Tab, or take a leak in private, or scream at someone to turn down the fucking stereo. In social studies Taylor had once told them of American soldiers held prisoner by the Japanese during World War II who had lost all hope of release, and actually willed themselves to death. After an hour of staring down the walls, she had decided that could happen to anybody.

She had to find a way out. She knew it was crazy —even her father would have problems getting out of here—but if she didn't have a scheme, and do something to fight these people, she was afraid of eventually becoming like those POWs and completely vegging out.

She searched the cell and found a dusty Bic pen beneath her cot. Hacksaw Jones, a notorious burglar who had escaped from several federal penitentiaries, had once corresponded with her father, envious of his record and hoping to learn a few things that might put him back on the street. Her father had written back, telling Hacksaw he'd be happy to exchange secrets after Hacksaw was paroled. In a subsequent letter Hacksaw had tipped some of the gems he wanted to impart when they met: he claimed that any non-electric cell door could be opened with the plastic cartridge from a pen. Her father had laughed at this, but right now Crystal was willing to try anything. She knelt in front of the cell door.

The lockplate had an unusual sliding bolt and looked impossible to pick. Sticking both hands through the bars, she wiggled the plastic cartridge vertically into the keyhole and jiggled it around. If this had been a pair of handcuffs, she'd look for the main spring to be at the left of the keyhole, about a quarter inch above it. She pressed forcefully and heard a distinctive click.

"Judas priest." She stood up, slid the door open. This was plain weird; she might have tried for weeks without hitting the spring just right. Someday, when she and her father were together, she'd have to tell him about this. She could see him bursting into laughter.

What now? Take a stroll, go outside for a breath of air? *Right*. Before she could decide, the cellblock door swung open, and two guards entered with their guns drawn.

"You know Rafael, I used to think you were sane," the warden declared, shuffling across the empty recreation yard toward the building that served as the prison's administrative offices. "It's hard for me to believe that you and I were once partners, and that you were someone I could trust." His foot sent a dull gray object skipping across the ground and he found it and picked it up. "Do you know what this is? The inmates call them 'shivs.' They make them in the machine shops. When I first came here, I had the guards thoroughly inspect every cell in the prison. Know how many shivs they found?"

"I have absolutely no idea," Guerra said, trying to keep pace with him.

"Nearly three hundred. It was staggering. If they'd taken on the guards, it might have been a fair fight. But no more, those days are over." He pounded his chest proudly. "Last week's inspection turned up five shivs and that's a lot. I run Santa Maria now. Not the inmates, not the guards. And not you, Rafael. Despite what you think, you had no right coming here."

"You act like I've done something wrong," Guerra said, taking a crumpled envelope with a government seal from his pocket. "Both women are under my protective custody. I needed some place safe to put them. I've broken no laws."

"Don't insult my intelligence." The warden halted, balled his fists, and squared off as if ready to go a few hard rounds. That was how he and Rafael had met, punching the heavy bag in the police gym. After they had sparred and bloodied each other's noses, they'd become friends. "Your relationship to the law is, at best, a nodding acquaintance. Even when you and I were pounding a beat, you placed yourself above it."

Guerra shoved his hands into his pockets, knowing better ways to fight. "I had nowhere else to turn. You and I were partners how long? Six years? I didn't think you'd—"

"Don't play on my emotions," the warden spouted indignantly. "I run this facility, and am personally responsible for the six hundred and thirty-two inmates. And now, in your wisdom, I have two more to look after; an undercover DEA agent and a teenage girl." His balled fists popped open, as if his fingers were exploding, and he raised them to the darkening sky. "There is nothing left for us to talk about. There is a gas pump located behind the mess hall. You can fill up your vans before you leave."

"Wait . . ."

"Goodbye, Rafael."

The warden unlocked a door to the administration

71

building and started to disappear when Guerra said, "We do have something to talk about."

"I'm afraid not," the warden said, going inside.

"*Money*," Guerra said. The door closed in his face. He stood in the courtyard and waited. Moments later the door reopened.

He heard the warden say, "How much money?"

"I can't see your face," Guerra told him.

The door opened fully. "I said—"

"I heard what you said. One million American dollars."

The warden's lips tightened. "To split?"

"All yours," Guerra said, seeing the man's eyes light up. One night fifteen years ago they had pulled an injured man out of a car wreck and found a roll of hundred dollar bills in his pocket. Still a rookie, Guerra had watched in fascination as his older partner had laid the injured man on the sidewalk, put a blanket over his face, and waited for his heart to stop.

"If you're joking with me . . ."

"It's on the level," Guerra said.

"Come in," the warden said, motioning him inside.

The warden's offices were located on the third floor of the administrative building and furnished like an expensive hotel suite. The subdued lighting and antique rosewood desk made Guerra feel as if he was inside the executive offices of a major corporation, and not the country's toughest prison. The warden offered him a seat with the wave of his hand, then plopped down in a dimpled leather swivel chair. Guerra remained standing, with his back to the picture window facing the barren courtyard. "This afternoon we were tailed. I took the girl out of the van, pretended I was going to shoot her. The men following us attempted a rescue."

The warden frowned. "Of the girl? Why?"

"What would you say if I told you that the girl was the agent, and the older women only a courier? I know. You would say, 'Rafael, you are snorting too much marching powder. One day you'll sneeze and your brains will fly out!' Nevertheless, I'm convinced it is true. She nearly slipped through our fingers at the hotel, and tried to escape again after we arrested her."

"I hope there's more," the warden said, unimpressed.

"The morning after Crystal Hardare was apprehended, two known CIA agents were seen in a car outside the Acapulco jailhouse. They were snapping pictures and taking notes."

The warden's frown grew deeper. "Why not the older woman? What is your infatuation with the girl?"

"It is not an infatuation," he said angrily. "The girl has been trained. She can open handcuffs without using keys. She used the cuffs to flatten one of my men with a single punch. Her father is a professional escape artist named Vincent Hardare. Many years ago, he helped rescue a young boy from a prison in Colombia, and no one at the prison claimed to have *seen* them." Putting his fists on the desk, he leaned forward. "Put the pieces together, my friend. Crystal is an agent. And two nights ago she received information that could put me, and all my people, out of commission. Wouldn't it seem logical that the CIA would sanction her father to rescue her?"

"Which is why you whisked both women out of

Acapulco, and brought them here," the warden concluded. Guerra nodded.

It sounded like lunacy, yet the warden accepted Guerra's evidence. With or without his sanity, he considered Rafael still the smartest street cop he'd ever known.

After a pause, he said, "I think your brain is fried."

The intercom on his desk buzzed. The warden picked up the phone, punching in a flashing light. "Yes?" His face turned to stone. Cupping his hand over the receiver, he said, "Two guards just found Crystal in her cell with the door open."

Guerra's dark eyes twinkled. "One of her many talents."

Into the phone he barked, "Change the lock." He hung up and let out a deep breath. "For a moment, let's suppose everything you say is true. What do you want me to do about it?"

"I want you to keep both women here," Guerra said.

The warden stood up, shaking his head. "Why? So her father can break in and rescue her?"

"*Attempt* to rescue her," Guerra said, now smiling. "Hardare will break in, and you, having been warned, will have set a trap, and will capture him. And then you will deliver him to the Colombian government, who will in turn pay you the tidy sum of one million dollars so they may put Hardare on trial for disgracing their penal system."

Their faces were inches apart. The warden stared, his eyes stone cold. "You have already spoken to the Colombians?"

"Yes."

The warden hesitated. "What if Hardare doesn't appear?"

Guerra reached into his inner breast pocket, removed a bulging envelope, and dropped it on the desk. "If I am wrong, then consider this a small token of my appreciation."

The warden used his forefinger to open the flap while quickly stealing a glance. Inside was a stack of hundred dollar bills nearly two inches thick. In his mind he did some quick calculations, then opened the desk drawer and slid the envelope inside. He came around the desk, put his hand on Guerra's back, and led him to the door. Before he opened it, he said, "I will be more than happy to help you, Rafael."

Guerra wrapped his arms around him. "I knew I could count on you," he whispered into his friend's ear.

Chapter 6

The Mercenary

*T*he phone woke him like a gunshot. His head snapped off the pillow, and he was instantly alert; outside it was still pouring rain, and the luminous clock on the night table read *11:40*. The phone rang again and he felt himself shudder. Friends never called this late, nor people you wanted so badly to hear from that the hour didn't matter. Just people with the worst news imaginable, or heavy-breathing cranks, or drunks who kept misdialing desperately trying to call their wives.

He started to switch on the lamp and wondered if it would be any easier to listen in the dark. It was certainly worth a try.

He answered on the next ring, fumbling with the receiver. "Hel . . ." His voice sounded old, rusty. "Hello." Heavy static, then nothing. "Who is this?"

A woman's voice spoke his name as if from the bottom of a well. Despite the bad connection he immediately recognized it; it belonged to Mrs. Hazel Darling, the headmistress at Rosemary Hall. He strained to hear her.

It was not any easier in the dark.

After hanging up, Hardare spent twenty minutes finding out where Richard Lyons lived. It wasn't easy; his home phone was unlisted, and the receptionist at the American embassy refused to give him the address. But Hardare was too angry to let himself become discouraged. He liked to think of himself as being resourceful. That morning he distinctly remembered seeing a copy of *The New York Times* on Lyons's desk, and felt safe in assuming that Lyons had it delivered to his home.

Directory assistance told him the name of the delivery service that handled the *Times*. That was easy, but what were his chances of catching anyone there? He dialed the number, let it ring twenty times before a sleepy girl with a Pakistani accent answered. He knew a few pleasantries in her native tongue, and quickly used them before she thought to question such a call at this hour of the night and slammed down the phone. Identifying himself as Richard Lyons, United States Ambassador to Great Britain, he complained that he hadn't gotten his *Times* in two weeks. Were they delivering it to his new address? The girl didn't know, and punched his name into a computer. Was he still living at 14 Craven Street, Covent Garden? Hardare knew the neighborhood well—it was, ironically, Crystal's favorite place to shop on Sunday afternoons—and he said yes, he was and hung up.

He threw on some clothes and took a cab to New Row in Covent Garden. The gaslight block was an odd melange of fruit wholesalers, trendy boutiques, and popular outdoor cafes, the sidewalks bustling with spiked and painted night people. Traffic started to crawl, and he abandoned the cab and walked the last few blocks to Craven Street.

It was a narrow, cobbled street filled with stately townhouses and tidy, postage-stamp plots of grass, and he found the mailbox for number 14 and went up the brick path. Inside the house he saw lights and heard the television and he pressed the front buzzer forcefully. Footsteps creaked in the hall, then the front door opened, still chained. A pretty woman, about thirty, stared at him. "May I help you?"

"I'd like to speak to your husband."

"You have the wrong—"

"No, I don't, Mrs. Lyons."

"Oh." She fixed her eyes on his face. "May I tell him who's calling at such an ungodly hour?"

Her tone was patronizing. "Vincent Hardare. The father of the girl whose life he fucked over this morning."

The door was slammed in his face. *You despicable*

man, he imagined her saying, fleeing inside. He waited on the stoop, and inside heard a heated exchange, doors slamming, and upstairs a little girl begin to wail. Moments later the front door reopened and Richard Lyons confronted him. He wore a terry bathrobe and slippers and smelled of a pipe. Hardare was happy that he'd gotten him from some place comfortable.

"You lunatic," he said, staring as if Hardare had just committed a murder. "How did you find out where I lived?"

Rain dripped down Hardare's face. "It was easy. I . . ." He stopped and smiled grimly. "I'm not as helpless as you think I am, Richard."

Lyons filled the doorway, his jaw tightening. "No, I don't suppose you are. What do you want?"

"The headmistress at my daughter's school called a half hour ago. She said Crystal was transferred to a maximum security prison outside Mexico City this afternoon. Said she'd heard it from your people. For Christ's sake, why didn't you call me?"

"Because I only found out an hour ago myself," Lyons explained, leaning against the door sill. "It's pretty late. I thought maybe you had heard enough bad news for one day."

A car passed on the street and splashed a puddle onto the flooding front lawn. Then Lyons's wife appeared in the foyer holding a portable telephone. "I can handle this myself," he said angrily, sending her back inside.

"I should never have listened to you," Hardare told him. "If I'd taken the Concorde to Miami this morning, I could have been in Acapulco before she was moved.

80

Do you have any idea how difficult it will be to break into a maximum security prison?"

Lyons squinted at him, the rain spotting his glasses. "You still want to help her? How? Stage a break-in of some kind?"

"Yes, and you're going to help me."

He wiped his glasses on his sleeve, considering. "You're more determined than I thought," he said, almost sounding apologetic. "All right. Go home, get some sleep. We'll talk first thing tomorrow."

"We'll talk now." There was a clap of thunder and the rain came down in sheets, drenching him. "I want a name."

Lyons slid his hand behind the door. "Whose name?"

"The name of someone—a mercenary—to back me up when I break into Santa Maria. Then you're rid of me—I'll take it from there."

"I can't get it for you now," Lyons insisted. "Why don't you go home, pour yourself a stiff belt, get some sleep?"

"No," Hardare said firmly. "I want the name *now*."

With that, Lyons shut the door in his face. His eye appeared in the peephole. "Call me at the embassy at eight."

Hardare took out his leather billfold, and with his American Express card effortlessly carded the door, pushing it open. Lyons stepped back as he entered the warm foyer. A puddle instantly formed at Hardare's feet, staining the carpet.

"Get out of my house, you crazy son of a bitch."

The door creaked eerily as rain blew in behind him.

"If you don't deliver now, I'll go. But I'll come back and open all the doors," he threatened. "I'll move the furniture around, turn the pictures upside down. I'm going to spook you. I know where you live, what your wife and two kids look like. You'll never feel—"

"No, you won't!" Lyons sprang forward in mid-sentence, his hands clasping Hardare's throat. For someone his size, his strength was unbelievable and Hardare found himself unable to breathe, his knees buckling. The foyer tilted on its axis, and just as the room began to spin he saw a bathrobed little girl fill the doorway and start to scream.

"Daddy, don't kill the man."

Lyons released Hardare and scooped his daughter up in his arms. Hardare leaned against the open doorway, still dizzy and unable to catch his breath.

"Daddy wasn't going to kill him," Lyons whispered to the child.

"Don't kid yourself," Hardare said, finding his voice. "You'd kill for *your* daughter if you had to."

"You're a persistent bastard, aren't you?" Lyons said.

"Yes."

"Go to bed, honey. It's all right." He stared at Hardare until the little girl was out of sight. "Wait here."

Lyons went into the house, leaving Hardare to dry out in the foyer, and Hardare heard him dial a telephone. When his call went through, he unexpectedly switched languages and rapidly spoke in what sounded to Hardare like Vietnamese. His conversation

82

was brief, and he returned to the foyer holding an unlit pipe.

"Be at Heathrow Airport in one hour," he said. "There's a cocktail lounge by the Pan American terminal. Sit at the second to last table from the bar."

"Who am I meeting?"

"An old bear named Frank Kincaid. He headed the S.O.G. in Vietnam—the Studies and Observation Group. Specialized in missions behind enemy lines. He's a hell of a soldier. If you don't believe me, just ask him. He's flying out of Paris tonight, has a short layover in London."

"Is he for hire?"

"Depends. He runs an anti-terrorist training school in Texas, sometimes does jobs on the side." He stoked his pipe with a disposable lighter, then puffed it amiably. "He's left his footprints in a lot of different places."

"You don't sound like a big fan."

Lyons shrugged. "I served under him."

"In the Army?"

"Green Berets."

Hardare felt something drop in the pit of his stomach. He'd just threatened and broken into the home of a man who could beat him to death with either hand. He wisely slipped out of the foyer and took several steps down the slippery path.

Tightening the knot in his robe, Lyons said, "I don't want you ever coming back here."

"Neither do I."

"Or harassing me or my family."

"You've got my word." A car passed and splashed a puddle onto the sidewalk.

"How do I find Kincaid?"

"You don't," Lyons puffed smugly on his pipe. "He finds you."

Heathrow was a desolate tomb. A few travelers staggered about, waiting for A.M. flights. Huffing as he ran past the deserted corridors and empty boarding gates, Hardare remembered one of his more unsettling nightmares. In it, he had died and gone straight to hell, and damnation was an endless airport terminal with no exits. For an eternity he had to walk around staring into the display windows of gaudy shops, eating processed and microwaved food, his boredom occasionally broken by the solicitation of a drum-beating Hare Krishna, or a blissed-out Moonie; two more lost souls.

It was after 2:00 A.M. when he entered a nameless cocktail lounge and sat at the designated table. The lounge was empty, and for a moment he thought the sight of a sweeper pushing a leisurely broom between the tables meant that the place was closing and that he had missed meeting Kincaid. But a sleepwalking waiter took his order and he sat back in his chair to wait.

He practiced making a blank matchbook disappear, palming it effortlessly in his left hand, then his right, meanwhile trying to imagine the man he was about to meet. He knew his name, a little of his background, but what was that worth? The English had an expression for mercenaries—they called them "whores of war"—and repeating it to himself made Hardare edgy, and conscious of the fact that he had absolutely no idea what he was getting into.

His drink came, mostly ice. He downed it and

winced. He heard what he thought was the waiter circling behind his table, and rattled the glass for his attention. "Another Gordon's and tonic, and easy on the ice. My nose is frozen."

"I'm not your fucking waiter," the man said, dropping a piece of Samsonite luggage at his feet. He sat down beside him, completely filling the chair. "Frank Kincaid. You had this overwhelming desire to meet me."

"Oh . . . right," Hardare stammered. "Would you like a drink?"

"Usually."

Hardare summoned the waiter and ordered another Gordon's for himself. "What would you like?"

"What's on draft?"

"Watney's, Guiness Stout, Becks, Heineken Dark, sir."

"What about American beer?"

"Sorry, sir."

"Give me a refreshing club soda, then."

When the man had left, Kincaid visibly relaxed, took out a pack of Luckies, and lit up. The cigarettes were unfiltered—Hardare hadn't seen anyone smoke them since high school—and as the match illuminated his rugged face, Hardare looked him over. Physically, Kincaid was about what he'd expected; in his early forties, a shade over six feet, muscular the way a farmer was muscular—in the back and shoulders. His face was leathery tan, his hair, probably brown originally but turned straw yellow by the sun. He might have passed for an aging lifeguard or a surfer, except for his eyes, which were a muddy green and never seemed to blink. He blew out the match.

"How much time do you have?" Hardare asked.

"Enough. Look, I didn't really want to meet you," Kincaid said in a surprisingly earnest tone. "Lyons told me about your kid, and it occurred to me that I didn't need any more headaches at this stage of my life. No offense, I'm sure your kid is great, but if she ends up getting hurt, or killed, I live with it too. Believe me." Hardare nodded; he did believe the man. "Then Lyons mentioned you were an escape artist, and sitting there in my skivvies in my hotel room I remembered something that I'd seen that blew my mind. A plane flying over Death Valley, a door opening, and some goddamn lunatic jumping out with his arms handcuffed behind him. You?"

"That's right."

"Took balls."

"Thanks."

"Mind if I ask you something?"

"It's free to ask."

Kincaid grinned, his lips two rigid lines. "Was it on the level?"

"You mean did I jump?"

"No, no. The cuffs, were they legit, or did you rap them," he hit his wrists against the tabletop, "and they flew off? I've seen those in novelty stores."

"They were regulation Smith and Wessons."

"No kidding. Shitfire and save matches." He inhaled on his cigarette implosively, leaned back in his chair, and for a moment seemed physically to sink into himself. The roar of a departing jet shattered the quiet of the lounge, and Hardare peered inquisitively through the haze of smoke, trying to read Kincaid's expression.

"I haven't seen your name in a while," Kincaid said after a pause. "Where have you been?"

There was no point in lying. Hardare said, "I was retired. Two years ago my wife was killed in a car accident. She used to assist me . . . since we were kids. Barbara was my wife, my assistant, my best friend, my business manager, and my biggest fan, all rolled into one. I lost all of that, and so I just quit the business." He stopped, his mouth very dry. A bothersome wisp of smoke curled off Kincaid's cigarette into his face. "Eventually I got over it, went back to work. It was a bad period."

"And stopped doing those escapes."

"The televised ones, yes. The last one was a month before the accident; I escaped from a safe dropped into San Francisco Bay." Their drinks came and Hardare dug out a few pounds and dropped the notes on the waiter's tray. Kincaid did not touch his club soda.

"Why did you stop?" he asked. "Lose your nerve?"

The question caught Hardare like a kick in the stomach, and he choked on his gin and tonic. Wiping his chin with a napkin, he said, "I risk my life every night I perform. That's part of being an escape artist. I live with it without too many problems."

"But that stuff is rehearsed," Kincaid argued. "You didn't practice jumping out of a plane wearing cuffs, did you?"

"Of course not," he said, the drink now empty in his hand. "Look, when Barbara died, my life turned upside down. Suddenly I had a fourteen-year-old kid on my hands. I didn't think it was fair to keep doing those escapes, and maybe make her an orphan."

"So you stopped for personal reasons."

"That's right. Look, there's a difference between retiring and quitting. I'm just as good now as I was then."

"Fine. Lyons said you were an expert at breaking into prisons. That's good, because I'm not. Unless you plan to use a dozen boys firing automatic weapons and throwing hand grenades." He laughed without smiling. "That, as they say, is *my* style. You want to break in with finesse, pick a few locks, be invisible, that sort of thing. Well, I can't do that without you by my side. And that means you might get caught, or shot full of holes. Most folks don't like the sound of that."

Kincaid paused, staring at him intensely. *Speak from your gut*, Hardare thought; *tell him how you feel right now, or he'll know you're lying*. "I'm as scared of dying as the next man. But do you know what scares me more? Never seeing my daughter again. I'll do whatever the hell is necessary to get her out of that prison alive and in one piece."

"That's what I needed to hear," Kincaid said.

"Good. Now let me make something clear to you. We are going to do this *my* way. We use my methods to go in, and my methods to get out. You are strictly back-up in case something goes wrong."

Kincaid's eyes narrowed. "Tell me exactly what you expect me to do."

"I want you to find out as much about Santa Maria prison as you can. A map of the area and aerial photographs would help. I also need a physical description of the prison's interior. After I put the plan together, I expect you to get any necessary equipment. You'll also be responsible for determining how to get both of us outside the front gates of Santa Maria without arousing suspicion. Breaking into the prison will be my job. I also want you to have an escape route planned once we leave the prison."

"You've really thought this out, haven't you?" Kincaid said.

"About a hundred times in the last 24 hours," Hardare replied.

Taking a sip of his club soda, Kincaid made a face and poured the soda into a plastic flower arrangement on the table. "Let's talk finances. You realize this isn't going to run cheap."

"How much?"

"My fee is sixty thousand dollars. You'll also have to pay for equipment plus my expenses. Figure eighty grand total."

Eighty thousand dollars! Hardare tried to hide his dismay. The mercenary that had freed Scott Weiner had charged the boy's father less than forty. But that had been almost ten years ago. "Sounds fair. Will that cover it all?"

"I think so."

"When do you want it?"

"I'm flying home to Texas tonight. Figure on flying in next Friday. You can bring it then."

Next Friday was nine days away, and in alarm Hardare said, "Can we afford to wait that long?"

"I don't know. But we can't engineer a break-in without first doing our homework. Even if you are an expert."

A flight announcement came over the public address and Kincaid removed his airline ticket and checked the departing time. "Got to head out," he said.

They stood up simultaneously with Kincaid offering his hand and Hardare clasping it. The soldier's handshake was firm and business-like, a contract consummated through a social gesture, and Hardare was grateful to him for offering the first glimmer of hope.

"One more thing. Don't talk to *anyone* about your daughter's situation. If this ever made the newspapers, it would be disastrous."

"I understand," Hardare said.

"Good. I'll call you the day after tomorrow." Kincaid raised his hand in a short salute, retrieved his suitcase, and left the cocktail lounge.

When he was gone, Hardare fell into his chair. He clasped his hand to his forehead and brought it away covered with perspiration. He hoped Kincaid hadn't noticed in the dim bar light. On a cocktail napkin he did some rapid arithmetic, and felt himself grow even warmer as he re-added the bleak sums.

He had blatantly lied to Kincaid. He didn't have eighty thousand dollars in the bank; he didn't even have one-third that amount. There was thirty thousand in his money market account, but half of that was needed to pay both his U.S. and U.K. income taxes, a necessary burden if he wished to remain an American citizen while living in London. He also owned a few hundred shares of dead-end stocks—he cursed his broker at E.F. Hutton, again—plus an IRA that brought his savings to a meager twenty-five thousand. The money simply wasn't there. He hadn't been drawing good salaries lately, and after paying Crystal's hefty tuition to Rosemary Hall, had found it impossible to save anything.

He balled the napkin in frustration. What in God's name was wrong with him? Only a few hours ago he'd threatened the family of an American diplomat, and now he'd hired a soldier of fortune with money he didn't possess. He wasn't just crazy, he was suicidal.

The waiter brought his change and Hardare left him half as a tip. Inside his wallet he found a grand total of ten pounds, enough for cab fare back to London. Nothing like starting out at the bottom, he thought.

Discarded baggage stubs littered the floor of the expansive Pan American terminal, and he kicked at them while searching for a solution. He needed to scratch up fifty-five thousand dollars in four days, which he supposed wasn't as ludicrous as it sounded. CBS had once paid him thirty thousand to escape from a burning house, while ABC, always the imitator, had coughed up forty grand for the airplane stunt. The money was out there; he just had to be clever enough to earn it.

Fifty-five thousand dollars.

Or seventy-five thousand before taxes.

In less than a week.

He took out his black address book and found Frank Stanley's unlisted home number. If any talent agent in London could swing him that kind of fee, Frank could. He found a pay phone and rang up his old friend.

He glanced at his watch. *2:20.* Last call at the pubs had been over two hours ago. *Come on Frank*, he implored as the line connected, *be home for once*. And still awake.

Chapter 7

Ten Percent

At ten the next morning, aging show biz impresario Frank Stanley held court in his posh Picadilly Square office to an immaculately attired Vincent Hardare. His friend looked like a million: new Armani suit, silk tie, his hair cut a bit shorter, giving him back a few years. *Wish I could do that*, Frank Stanley thought, firing up the day's first cigar. *Wish I still had some hair.*

He had his secretary hold his calls, gazed fondly at his gleaming friend across the desk, and began. "Vincent, you were blessed at birth. Really. You inherited your father's dramatic flair. When that man walked on a stage it was like a bolt of lightning sent down from the sky. He had *it*. Myself personally, I was also blessed; God gave me the eye for spotting talent. I remember one day . . ."

Oh no, Hardare thought, squirming uncomfortably in his wool suit; Frank was floating down Memory Lane. He could be as boring as a broken record, but Hardare supposed he was entitled; fifty years of hustling acts into London's better clubs and variety halls had made him something of an institution. Hardare crossed his legs and forced a smile.

". . . seeing this female dream in the paper. It wasn't a photo—just a pencil sketch, an ad for department store jewelry. But the girl's face, it was burning up the page. You know the look. Sultry but innocent."

"Sure," Hardare said, doing his best to act interested.

"I phoned the paper, got the ad agency's number. They told me the artist's name; he told me the modeling firm. An hour later I got her on the phone. 'This is Frank Stanley, the agent. I saw you in the paper, want to do a photo session?' Well, she laughed in my face! Said Frank Stanley the agent wouldn't waste his time calling a shopgirl in Bristol, and hangs up. Think I got sore? Only enough to hop into my car and hit Bristol. That afternoon I found her, signed her to an exclusive contract. The find of the century."

Hardare said, "Someone famous?"

"You won't believe this," his agent said impressively. "Carol Chesbro."

"Really?" The name drew an utter blank. He was

totally stumped. He said, "Wow, no kidding. What a break."

"One of my greatest discoveries. What an actress, a true starlet." Frank Stanley sighed stertorously and let his eyes shut, the memory a pleasant escape. "God, did I adore that kid. When she died I cried like a baby."

Only then did the name register. Carol Chesbro had gone down in a flaming airplane just outside Los Angeles in the late 1950s. Hardare vaguely recalled her— a tempting blonde, great legs, with a voice that purred—but he couldn't remember a single film she'd starred in. Too bad, that would have made points with Frank. He waited for his agent's melancholy to subside, then removed an envelope from his inner breast pocket. When he looked up he saw Stanley staring hard at him.

"What's in the envelope, Vincent? Looks long enough to be your will."

Hardare blinked at him. "Let's hope not."

"Should I read it?"

"In a minute. But first hear me out. I have a proposition for you."

Frank Stanley smiled approvingly. He was always willing to hear a creative sales pitch. "Start the music," he said encouragingly.

Hardare stood up, put the envelope on the desk. "Back in 1970, when I was getting started, breaking the act in here in England and France, I came to see you. My father said you were the best agent on the continent. So you and I had lunch, and you gave me some advice that I've never forgotten."

"I did?"

"You said magicians were outdated, and couldn't

compete with television or the movies. To be successful, I had to make myself legitimate to the public, and prove I deserved using Houdini's name in my billing. I took your advice, and staged a series of escapes for the press. I started to get bookings, and you suggested making the escapes more death-defying. Remember my first big stunt? A locked house loaded with dynamite. Six seconds after I got out the joint blew up; they found parts of the roof over a mile away."

"Scared living hell out of me," his agent admitted.

"Of course it did, Frank. More people saw that escape on the news than saw Houdini perform in his entire career. I made my name with that escape, and the ones that followed." Picking up the envelope, he placed it into his agent's hands. "I've got something new. Better than all the others. And I want you to sell it."

"I hate to bring up a painful subject," his agent said, removing three folded sheets of neatly typed paper, "but I thought you gave the crazy stuff up. Something about not being able to get life insurance . . ."

"I did," Hardare admitted, moving animatedly around the office, his eyes avoiding his own father's picture grouped with several others on the wall, "and it hurt my career. To stay popular, I have to make headlines." He pointed his finger dramatically at the proposal. "This one escape will generate more publicity than an army of press agents could drum up in a year."

Frank Stanley felt his enthusiasm mounting. Only a few short years ago Vincent had been the hottest variety act in the business. Why not again? "Is this something we can sell to a cable TV outfit? They're paying top dollar for special events."

"Absolutely," Hardare said. Stanley slipped on his

bifocals and started to read, and Hardare retired to his chair and clasped his hands in his lap.

"The Jaws of Death," the agent mumbled. "You've even got a bleeding name for it."

"I was in a creative mood," Hardare said.

The memory was a peculiar thing. Frank Stanley had always liked Vincent's father, David, but it had taken him nearly ten minutes to remember what had initially impressed him. It was during a lavish dinner at a private club in London a few years before the war with Hitler. The roomful of men were well into the brandy and cigars when someone spoke up and asked David what the most difficult part of escaping from the icy Thames had been just a week before. The room had grown silent. Staring into space, David had responded in his most serious tone.

"Most people think not drowning is the hardest part," he said, "because the water is so unbearably cold." He puffed on his cigar. "Others think it's impossible to escape from the dozen pair of handcuffs and leg irons that bound my wrists and ankles together, especially beneath the water." For a moment he let the brandy swirl in his snifter. "But the *most* difficult part, to tell the truth, was jumping in the water."

"Jumping in the water," the man repeated.

"Very difficult," David said, turning so he was staring fully at the man. "You see, it was freezing cold standing on that dock in a bathing suit, and I knew it would be even *colder* when I jumped in. And thinking about it made it worse. I was paralyzed."

By now the man was on the edge of his seat. A waiter passed the table and refilled David's snifter. David sampled the offering, nodded approvingly. Very good, he mumbled.

"But why did you jump in if you were so terrified?" the man had finally blurted out.

"I didn't," David had replied. "My agent pushed me."

That was David. In the son Stanley saw traces of the father, but also weaknesses, and a run of bad luck. His losing Barbara had been the crushing blow. She was an elegant woman—a vision in black and pearls on stage—and as much a support to her husband as a foundation is to a house. He looked across the desk sympathetically. "Vince, no one wants good fortune for you more than me. Sure, the bookings have been lean. But they'll pick up; I heard the bird act is really coming along."

"You don't like it." He nodded at the proposal.

"Like it? It's total lunacy." Stanley tossed the papers into Hardare's lap. "Sharks have been known to eat people."

"Come on, Frank," Hardare insisted, "you could pick up the phone and sell this in five minutes."

"Probably."

"Then what's stopping you?"

"My memory." He held up his hand. "Just listen. Right after you lost Barbara, something inside of you died. I know that, and you know that. And if you don't believe me, look at the act you're doing now, and the one you were doing two years ago."

"Frank . . ."

"Forget about the crazy escapes. Just do the

magic—it's a living. We all change, Vincent. Why can't you accept that?"

"Because I need the money," he said, nearly whispering, his body slumped in his chair. "And I need it fast."

"Then I'll lend it to you," his agent said hurriedly, pulling a checkbook from a desk drawer. "You can have it in your hands in fifteen minutes."

"I can't take your money," Hardare insisted.

"Why not? I've been stealing from you for years. Part of the business."

Hardare laughed hollowly; it was good to know who his friends were. "I need sixty thousand dollars. By Friday."

Stanley dropped the checkbook. "Are you out of your tiny mind? What kind of trouble are you in?"

Hardare shook his head. Kincaid had warned him not to talk about his daughter's situation, and he could think of no one worse to confide in than a booking agent, even if he was a friend and had once managed his father.

"You'll get a straight ten percent commission," Hardare said. "Plus a twenty-five percent take on any money we pick up for closed circuit or cable TV rights."

"Who will pick this up on such short notice?"

"Tourist season for the big resort hotels in Blackpool is coming up. With the publicity from this, they wouldn't have to advertise for a year." Hardare paused. "I need an answer now, this morning."

"Then the answer is no." Frank Stanley spoke slowly and emphatically. "The risks are too great. I'd be signing your death certificate. No amount of money in the world will make me do that."

An oppressive silence fell over the office. On the

walls the faces of stars of a bygone era smiled expectantly, their eyes filled with confidence, and hope, and dreams yet unfulfilled.

"What are you saying, Frank?"

"Do I have to spell it out?" he replied, clenching his liver-spotted hands into fists. "You might get killed. You don't have any life insurance. What will happen to your daughter? I don't want that on my conscience."

Hardare's jaw quivered. "You think I'm washed up."

"I didn't say that."

"You know I can pull this off, Frank." Hardare stuffed the proposal into his jacket, went to the door. "My father nearly suffocated once trying to escape from a steel can filled with whiskey. Think anyone stopped booking him? No one did, not even you." He angrily tugged on his gloves, then pulled a long list from his pocket. "There are ten other agents in town who'll be more than happy to represent me."

"Then why did you come here?" Stanley snapped, losing his temper. "They don't bloody care if you get killed."

"Because I'd rather do business with you," Hardare said, opening the door. "I didn't come here for advice. I'm doing the escape—it's up to you if you want to book it."

"Of course I do. It's just . . ." Stanley hesitated. From a purely business angle Frank Stanley knew he was making a huge mistake. "The Jaws of Death" would undoubtedly cause a worldwide sensation, and would be easy to sell. He could call it "The Return of the World's Greatest Escape Artist." If Vince wasn't willing to be talked out of it, then why shouldn't Frank represent him? He stood to make a tidy sum; if he didn't, another agent would, and that galled him. "Let me think about it."

"Sure." Hardare held the door open. "Well?"

"Well, what?"

"You thought about it. What's your decision?"

"Well, all right. But I pray I don't live to regret it."

Hardare rushed across the office and grasped his arm appreciatively. "You're a lifesaver, Frank."

"Get out of here, before I change my mind."

The office door slammed shut, a sheet of white note-paper blowing off the desk. Frank Stanley retrieved it and stared at the words he'd written earlier across the top: *THINGS TO DO TODAY*.

Picking up a ballpoint, he wrote in large capital letters across the middle of the page: *GET YOUR HEAD EXAMINED*.

Then he picked up the phone and went to work.

For an hour Hardare pounded the sidewalks of Picadilly Circus, not wanting to go home and stare at the phone. Walking usually rejuvenated him, and after an hour of navigating the twisting streets he felt better than he had in days.

At noon he ducked into a restaurant to use the phone. He called his answering service, and while on hold, an alert waitress read him the lunch menu. A hot meal sounded good, and he ordered a cup of split pea soup, fresh rolls, the day's special, which was shepherd's pie, and tea. The waitress smiled, tickled that an American would order a typical English meal.

"You have two calls," he heard the operator say. "Mr. Richard Lyons at 42-9752. The other from Frank Stanley. He says you know the number."

Hardare hung up, waited for the waitress to leave, then dialed Lyons's number, surprised Lyons would contact him after their ugly encounter the night before.

"I've been trying to reach you all morning," Lyons said, his voice sounding tinny on the conference phone.

Hardare tensed up. "With good news or bad?"

"No, nothing new. Look, I was a little hard on you last night. You've been under a tremendous strain. How did your meeting with Kincaid go?"

He hesitated. "We talked."

"That's all?"

"He wants a lot of money, more than I have on hand. It's going to take a few days to scratch up."

"How much?" Lyons asked, and before Hardare could answer added, "If you're strapped for funds, maybe the government can arrange a loan."

"No, but thanks anyway. I don't want a loan, especially one I might not be able to pay back. Call me if you hear anything," he said, then hung up.

Frank Stanley did have news. "I've got somebody nibbling at the bait," his agent said. "They're on the other line. Call me back in ten minutes."

He hung up. A steaming cup of tea awaited him at the table. "I thought you might need this," his waitress said. He did. Taking a deep sip before he sat, he smiled, and gave the startled girl a kiss on the cheek.

*　*　*

"You were going to hit him up," Lyons said in disbelief. He was in his real office, tucked away in the catacombs of the embassy, the walls painted with lead to prevent eavesdropping. "That's why you poured your drink over our bug in the flowerpot. So we wouldn't hear you giving Hardare a bill."

"I had to be sure he was serious," Kincaid said, admiring a posed photo on the wall of Lyons enthusiastically pressing the flesh with Ronald Reagan. Kincaid wore black pants and a baggy fisherman's net sweater, his clothes making him look like the captain of a trawler. "Maybe he was just shooting off his mouth. I had to find out."

"How much?"

Kincaid turned, acting distracted. "Come again."

"You heard me."

"Sixty thousand. Plus expenses."

"Sweet fuck. You're a real prince, aren't you?"

"No, I'm not, and stop acting like you're going to have a shit-hemorrhage." He folded his arms and leaned comfortably against the imitation hardwood desk. "This is a free-lance job, remember, no strings attached. I'm entitled to make money any way I please. Besides, you think he was expecting I'd help him for free? Get real. Sixty is a fair price. Anyone else would charge him seventy-five thou, even a hundred to go into Mexico."

"Where's he going to find someone else?"

"Where have you been? In a cave?" Discovering a candy dish on the desk, Kincaid pilfered several striped mints. "Pick up a copy of *Soldier of Fortune* and take a peek at the classifieds. Plenty of goons for hire."

Lyons shook his head. "What if he can't come up with it?"

"Let him rob a bank. Look, you said Hardare wanted to hire a mercenary. If he needs money, let him get motivated. Now let me see what you've got." He popped a mint into his mouth while Lyons opened a manila envelope and extracted several black and white glossies. The first showed two women kneeling on a road, one a blonde teenager, the other in her late twenties, nice face. A man in uniform who looked to be straight out of Central Casting—olive-brown skin, thick mustache, sleeves rolled up to his elbows—was holding a gun against the older woman's head, and Kincaid could tell right away he was not planning to pull the trigger. Too distracted. "Who took these. Your people?" Lyons nodded. "Guy with the gun is the one you were telling me about. What's his angle?"

"Name's Guerra. Two years ago, he was promoted to zone commander in Mexico's massive anti-drug war, and was put in charge of a fleet of helicopters and a few dozen men. Instead of arresting the drug barons in his zone, Guerra took over their operations, then murdered them. He currently controls about one-third of the heroin and coke coming out of Mexico."

"Why did he nab your girl?"

"Maria had infiltrated his network. She was close to finding out how he made his shipments, which would have destroyed him."

"How much about your operation in Mexico did Maria know about?"

"Enough. Names, faces. We've already pulled our better people off the street, just to be safe."

Kincaid crunched the mint in his mouth. "You'd probably be better off if he killed her. No more liability."

"He's not that stupid." Lyons showed him several

aerial photographs of Santa Maria Penitentiary. "This is where he's keeping them. We can't go in unless we use an army."

"And armies usually start wars. Mind if I keep these?" He put the photographs back into the envelope, tucking them under his arm. "How does Hardare's kid figure into this?"

Lyons shrugged his shoulders. "We don't know. We're guessing she was in the wrong place at the wrong time."

"You're guessing? Come on, you can do better than that."

"You make it sound like you don't trust me, Sarge."

"Guerra didn't grab Hardare's kid because he likes the way she smells. Your people are keeping tabs on Guerra, tapping his phones. You must know what he's thinking."

"We honestly have no idea," Lyons said, a hint of resentment in his voice. "But rest assured Frank, if we find out, you'll be the first to know."

Kincaid got his pea coat, went to the door. "I'm flying out this afternoon. I'll call you once I hear from Hardare." He paused. "Mind if I give you some advice, Richie?"

"What's that?" Lyons said stiffly.

"Can the picture of Ronnie. Everyone's got one."

"It's autographed."

"So's mine. Later."

Chapter 8

The Jaws
of Death

I n one of his many magic books, Houdini had written "There are two types of escapes. Those an audience forgets five minutes after seeing, and the ones they remember the rest of their lives. Escape artists cannot simply *escape*. First there must be recognizable danger, then a struggle, and finally freedom. It is like a Greek tragedy, and if the escape artist can convince the audience that he has miraculously cheated death, then he has succeeded."

Hardare had designed "The Jaws of Death" with these guidelines in mind. Over the years, he had made a study of human fears and phobias, and finding the single greatest fear held by people around the world, went about incorporating it into an escape. The end result was a routine that he could perform only once, and never would want even to think about again.

Since its announcement in the London newspapers over a week before, it had amassed more TV time and columns of newspaper space than all of his previous escapes combined. He had also received sackfuls of telegrams, some from complete strangers wishing him luck, others from crackpots prophesying his demise, and a few hundred from concerned magicians who understood the risk he was taking, and begging him to reconsider the possible consequences.

Their concern centered around a single fact. Never before had an escape artist challenged another living creature, especially one so hostile toward human beings. If the escape backfired, there was no hope of saving Hardare, no chance of survival.

This time, he'd outdone himself. The ultimate opponent for the ultimate test.

The shark.

Hardare tilted the Venetian blinds with a finger and gazed with reluctant fascination at the spectacle five floors below. Down on the great lawn beside the swimming pool a four-piece electric jazz band was belting out old favorites while waitresses served mixed drinks at two pounds a hit to the buzzing mob of spectators and cliquish newspaper reporters. For a moment his view of the pool was unobstructed, and he stared at the dancing orange stars in the water's still surface. Despite being booked to capacity, the hotel's pool had not been swum in since the day before, and the salt water was fresh and sparkling clean. A soft knock on the door.

"Come in."

It was Frank Stanley. He wore a polo shirt and Bermuda shorts, his milk-white legs looking like skinny poles. "Everything's set. Cable people are all hooked up."

"Right." Hardare slipped into a black robe and noticed his agent staring reproachfully at the bathing trunks he was wearing.

"I thought you decided on the black ones," Stanley said.

"The blue look less somber. Let's go." They started to leave when Stanley crossed the room to switch off the droning TV. On the screen Hardare saw Robert Shaw giving Paul Newman a murderous look, and realized he was watching one of his favorite scenes from the movies, the crooked poker game in *The Sting*. Hardare had a sudden, painful dèjá vu. Las Vegas, ten years ago, the free-fall straitjacket escape. Walking out of the hotel room and noticing what was on the TV his daughter was watching . . .

"Oh no," Barbara had said, standing behind him in the open door. "And that's your favorite part of the movie. Shaw switches in his own deck, which is already set up."

"He brings in a cooler," Hardare had said quietly.

"But Newman is on to him," she'd gone on, nuzzling the back of his neck with soft kisses, "and switches out his good hand for an even better one."

"Switches his hand at the same instant he sneezes into his necktie. Perfect misdirection."

Very quietly she'd asked him, "Are you scared?"

"A little."

"How many littles?"

"A lot."

"Well, don't be," Barbara said, mocking anger. "That's my job. You do the escapes and leave the worrying to me."

He had laughed loud enough for two people.

"You say something Vincent?"

Hardare blinked. He didn't answer. His eyes swept the gaudy hotel suite with its king-sized bed and tastelessly mirror-paneled walls. A feeling had overcome him a few hours earlier, and he had wondered if it was the fear of dying. Now he realized that was only part of it; mostly it was the fear of dying alone.

"You sure you're feeling okay?" Frank Stanley said.

"Sure."

They took an elevator to the main lobby. Counting the floors, he heard his agent say, "You can still back out."

Hardare scowled at him.

"Say you cut yourself shaving."

"Right. And spend the rest of my career in Montreal."

They went from the lobby outside to the pool area. Four beefy hotel guards escorted him through the throngs of media people, and Hardare proceeded with head bowed, ignoring the microphones thrust inches from his face. A cheer arose from the balconies and he looked up. The hotel had fifteen floors, twenty suites per floor, with people jammed on the balconies like sardines stacked in a can. From one balcony hung a colored banner which read: *HARDARE 1—SHARKS O.* He liked the score, and waved.

At poolside he kicked off his sandals and stuck his toe into the water. The pool was twelve feet deep, big enough to hold over two hundred bathers, and had been fitted with a steel gate at the deepest end. On the other side of the gate, in a holding pen, he saw the water's surface cut by the exposed dorsal fins of three tiger sharks.

His worthy opponents. Ugly animals, each over ten feet long, weighing close to two hundred pounds. Two days before a Spanish fisherman had caught them in the Mediterranean when they attacked his catch of dolphin and became ensnared in his nets. Tiger sharks were natural predators, and would swim endlessly in circles for hours, waiting for their next meal. Eating, Hardare had realized, was the only thing they really enjoyed doing.

Frank Stanley helped remove his robe. "You ready?"

"Why not?"

"Oh, I can think of a thousand reasons."

In the crowd he spotted a silver-haired gentleman wearing a navy blue blazer and charcoal gray slacks, and moved to make space for the man many considered England's top television commentator.

"Good to see you," said Larry Muldare, warmly clasping his hand. He was staid yet handsome, with a

111

pencil-thin mustache and slight gap marring his front teeth, and he got down to business without hesitation. "The cameras will be rolling in a minute. I'll do the intro the way we rehearsed it this morning, unless there's something you'd like to add."

Hardare recalled little of their rehearsal except that Muldare had acted mildly hungover. "Please remember one thing."

Muldare raised his eyebrows. "Yes. . . ?"

"This is for real. No mirrors, no inflated sharks in the pool. If I don't get out, I get eaten."

"God help us if you don't get out," he mumbled under his breath. Suddenly Muldare's people swarmed over them, with two mobile cameras focusing on Muldare, and a technician began a ten-second countdown. A hush fell over the area. Hardare stared down at his toes and felt surprisingly relaxed. The weather was perfect, the hotel packed, his money already in the bank. He looked at his blue trunks, wished he'd worn the black pair. Someone said, "Ready" and he glanced up into the glowing red eye of a television camera.

"Good afternoon, I'm Larry Muldare, coming to you live from the Seascape Resort in Blackpool, England. We're here today to witness what many concede is the most difficult challenge ever attempted by one man.

"To my left stands Vincent Hardare, renowned escape artist and nephew of Harry Houdini. In the next few minutes, he will be locked in handcuffs, sealed inside a packing case, and lowered into a swimming pool." He paused while the empty pool was flashed on the monitors. "After Hardare enters the pool, three man-eating tiger sharks will be released into the water. Hardare will attempt to escape in full view, and risk certain death.

"During the past few days, many have doubted the authenticity of this escape. Some thought the sharks would be drugged, or missing their teeth. A short while ago I had the opportunity to examine the sharks up close, and let me assure you, they are anything but docile."

On the monitor Hardare watched a film of the tiger sharks devouring a large chunk of raw meat, their jaws clacking feverishly. The picture switched back to Muldare. "Hardare, I realize this is a tense moment, but are there any thoughts you'd care to share with us?"

"Yes, there are," he said, forcing a smile. "Human beings are naturally inhibited by phobias. Selachiophobia, the fear of sharks, is one of the greatest. The reason I am performing the "Jaws of Death" is the same reason I perform all my escapes. I want to show people there is no fear that cannot be overcome."

Muldare seemed absorbed by his statement. "That's quite remarkable. For everyone's sake, let's hope you succeed."

On cue, two policemen stepped up and snapped three gleaming pairs of handcuffs to Hardare's wrists. They escorted him across the lawn to an open packing case, and as he stepped in, Muldare pressed him for a final remark. "Anything before we start?"

"I'd like to thank everyone for turning out on such short notice," he said, raising his manacled wrists to the balconies. "And also the Seascape Resort. I'd also like to say hello to my daughter, wherever she is."

With a grim smile, Muldare said, "Good luck."

"Thanks." He crouched down, and the lid was fitted and nailed shut. The four hotel guards hoisted the case by its corners, and shuffled slowly toward the pool. Perspiring heavily, Frank Stanley trudged alongside them.

"Vincent, you okay?" he asked through an air hole.

From inside a voice said, "One thing."

"What's that?"

"Tell me I'm not fucking crazy."

"You're not fucking crazy."

"Thanks. I had myself scared."

Two of Hardare's assistants were in the pool treading water, and as the case was lowered between them, they carefully guided it to the pool's center. As the case began sinking, their movements rippled across the gate to the enclosed end of the pool, and a shark butted its nose against the steel barrier. When the packing case hit bottom, the two assistants made a deliberate exit from the water.

Next to the pool a giant clock was set in motion— a trademark of any Hardare escape—and after ten seconds elapsed one of the assistants yelled "*Let's do it!*" and the gate was slowly lifted.

The sharks entered the open area cautiously, bumping the walls. The water magnified their size, and up on the hotel balconies the crowd turned still, sobered by the start of something that no one knew how would end.

As the first tiger shark circled the pool, its dorsal fin could be heard slicing the water with a soft hissing sound.

Holding his breath, Hardare sat in a fetal curl, the handcuffs already off, lying at his feet. The sharks were above him, and he felt water pour through the air holes in the crate. Using a steel shim taped to his right sole, he pried open two boards, and peered out. Bright television lights illuminated the water, and he saw a shark pass a foot from the case, its ferocious gullet wide open.

He watched the creatures circle overhead. His assistant had dropped the gate to the holding pen, and it was here that the secret of the escape was hidden. The gate was gimmicked, with a trap door in the bottom that could be easily sprung.

On paper the escape was simplicity itself. Opening the crate with the shim, he'd swim twenty-two feet across the bottom, spring the trap door, and swim into the holding pen. Behind the holding pen was a small hole that led to one of the pool's large purifying pumps. The pump had been removed, and the hole widened to allow Hardare to swim through. Two of the bars on this side of the pen could be unscrewed, allowing him to pass through the hole and swim straight up, emerging behind a large concession tent without being seen by the cameras or the crowd. Someone on the top floor of the hotel might see him, especially if he or she had binoculars. But he wasn't worried. Exposing the escape to a handful of people wasn't a concern so long as a few million were fooled.

Very simple, except for the sharks. If they sensed his presence in the water, they might attack, and he'd taken great precautions to keep them distracted, and as far away as possible.

In planning his escape, he'd consulted a top marine biologist, and learned that most shark attacks occur in tropical waters, which had prompted him to have the pool water chilled. Sharks also had the most acute hearing of any fish, and with the biologist's help he had constructed an underwater amplifier and hidden it in the pool's massive purifying pump.

In over a hundred tests the amplifier had successfully drawn the sharks to a neutral area of water. Most sharks were totally blind, and "saw" sonically through microscopic sensors hidden beneath their sandpaperlike skin. Turning on the amplifier was like holding up a jar of honey to a bear. And when the sharks swam in one direction, he would swim in the other.

The rest was pure theater. Once out of the pool, he'd run around the hotel to the police helicopter waiting in the parking lot, have himself strapped in a lifeline and carried up over the hotel. The helicopter would lower him over the pool, where he'd dangle a few feet above the sharks and wave to the crowd. Actually it was pure showmanship, but people loved that kind of thing, and if he made it out alive, hell, he'd love it too.

But before all this occurred, he had to wait. Making people worry was the key to building tension; his audience needed time to let their imaginations run wild. With each passing second of the clock their anxiety would mount. Soon they'd be believing he'd run out of air, and had drowned.

He checked his watch. Sixty seconds had passed. In another minute the amplifier would be activated by an assistant sitting behind the tents, and he'd pry open the case and start swimming. Until then, he was content to sit still, and let his thoughts wander.

Up at poolside things were not so calm.

Standing on the great lawn, Frank Stanley could tell the party was over. Everyone around him, including the drunken parties up on the balconies, had grown deathly quiet. The tiger sharks were big, frightening animals, and the water's magnification made them look even larger, almost mammoth. They were also fast, darting down the length of the pool in seconds. The first time they did, a woman on an upper balcony had shrieked.

That had sobered everyone up. Then the electric jazz band had stopped playing, and Frank Stanley had grown worried; if the escape was a dud, the real trick might be getting out of town. Edging up to the bar, he motioned for a refill, and holding a Beefeater to his lips, caught a dirty glare from a bearded photographer standing beside him. Stanley turned his back and drank, now gazing at the pool. He could remember wakes where he'd had a better time.

For ten million viewers watching on cable television, the waiting wasn't so unbearable. Larry Muldare was doing his inimitable best to keep things lively, and as the seconds expired he highlighted Hardare's colorful career as an escape artist. Muldare's cultured voice was unusually calm, yet in front of the camera, sweat poured off the end of his nose. The cameraman focusing on him wisely pulled back.

If one person in the crowd wasn't nervous, it was a forty-year-old Californian named Michael Cribbins. A respected magician and illusion maker, Cribbins had designed many of Hardare's better escapes, and often assisted him during his televised stunts. Today he was hidden behind the bar near the pool, a powerful transmitter in his lap. When the giant clock next to the pool reached two minutes, he would activate the transmitter and draw the sharks to the purifying pump, letting Vince escape.

Ten seconds left. Cribbins stole a peek around the bar. The sharks were swimming faster than before, as if something directly above their heads had upset them. Cribbins could sense it too, and it was emanating from the crowd. *Despair!*

These people didn't know Vince, Cribbins thought, leaning back comfortably against the bar. His earlier stunts had been more dangerous than this. Maybe the accident had changed him—who wouldn't be changed after seeing his wife burn to death?—but the reflexes were still there, Cribbins wouldn't have agreed to help if they weren't. One way or another, Vince would get out of the pool alive.

Time! He flipped the switch and stole another peek around the bar. Almost immediately the sharks began thrashing the water with their tails, soaking several cameramen trying to get a closer shot. The men jumped back, and the sharks made a bee-line to the purifying pump. Cribbins felt elated. Everything was working perfectly.

The sharks' frenzied actions triggered an immediate response. On the top floor of the hotel a woman pouring champagne screamed. "He's being eaten alive," her voice announced, piercing the air like a siren. She swayed uncertainly on the balcony, and a man wisely threw his arms around her. Another woman let out a scream, then another, and a man with a German accent bellowed, "For God's sake, someone help him before he dies!" His cry acted as a catalyst, and the screams and pleas quickly escalated, fueling their own hysteria. Down at poolside Larry Muldare could not hear himself speak.

The great lawn became a stadium of deafening noise. For the sharks, it was equivalent to setting off a depth charge, and they thrashed around the pool, savagely butting their heads against the tiled walls. In a fit of rage, one bit down on the pectoral fin of the shark beside it, severing it completely. The injured animal swam to the pool's center, trailing a dark stream of blood.

His two companions blindly pursued, ripping into him with a cannibalistic fury. The water turned dark red, splashing in huge waves across the lawn. It was a gruesome scene—with the shredding sounds reaching the top floor of the hotel—and the photographers and cameramen fought for room around the pool edge.

Michael Cribbins appeared from behind the bar. He had tried to turn the transmitter off, hoping it would calm the sharks down. Instead he had broken it, and now could see the amplifier actually making tiny waves in the water. *God, no!*

His blazer soaked, Larry Muldare ducked beneath a tent and screamed into his microphone. "Somebody do something! This is horrible . . . I don't know—shoot the goddamned sharks if you have to!"

Frank Stanley could not move. He watched the pool turn black, then silently said good-bye to his friend. He raised his drink and finished it.

The giant clock read: *Two minutes twenty seconds.*
Hardare had begun his escape.

He was out of the packing case and swimming
across the pool bottom, admiring his own ingenuity,
when there was a tremendous disruption in the water.

A torrent of air bubbles escaped his lips. The three
tiger sharks had suddenly converged above him and
started attacking one another. One shark flipped over
repeatedly, its tail wildly slapping the water. Then the
amplifier went crazy—the buzzing made his ears ring
—and he felt his heart pounding in his head.

He tried to swim away and the sharks swept over
him, turning the water darker than night. In desperation
he lay completely still and tried to determine where the
sharks were, and exactly where he was in relation to
the canal. As he started to swim again, a tail whipped
across his shoulders, and more air bubbles escaped. He
shut his eyes, waiting for the teeth to sink in.

Nothing. He opened his eyes, unable to see twelve
inches in front of his face. Where was the gate? He had
no idea. He beat his fist angrily against the floor, his
lungs ready to explode. In his excitement he'd burned
up much of his oxygen; very soon, against his will, his
brain would command his mouth to open, and he would
start swallowing water. I can't die here, he thought. If
he died in Mexico that was one thing; at least he could
draw his last breath knowing he had tried. But dying
here was meaningless. And he'd go out a failure . . .

What was left? Prayer? What should he ask for?
Strength, forgiveness. The water grew darker, his vision

fading. Then, very clearly, he saw his daughter; she was dressed in faded blue jeans and a dirty T-shirt and sitting on a metal cot in a tiny prison cell. Her dark-ringed eyes had a distant, empty look. He had seen that empty gaze before in prisons around the world; it was a look of despair and of pain and of all hope lost.

Hardare opened his eyes. If I die here, he thought, that is how I will spend the rest of eternity remembering Crystal.

He had one other choice. He could surface, get air, get his bearings, and dive back down. The sharks would sense him instantly, he knew that, but he hoped they would be preoccupied with killing each other. What a choice!

He braced himself. Just break the surface, take a big gulp, and come back down. Hell, if he survived, freeing Crystal from jail would seem easy. The thought was oddly comforting, and he immediately propelled himself off the pool bottom.

He broke the surface to the sound of a thousand screams. Sucking down air, he saw the gate twenty feet to his right, then a man from the cable TV company frantically waving his arms, urging him to go back down. Hardare realized he was in danger and thought: *You shouldn't have told me.*

Turning his head slowly, Hardare stared into the ferocious open gullet of the largest tiger shark. It was close enough to touch. He froze in the water and stared at its double rows of teeth. *The end.*

The shark edged forward, butting Hardare's chest, then closed its jaws and slipped beneath the surface. Hardare's heart leaped. The animal was dead.

The crowd roared as Hardare went under.

He touched bottom and felt a sandpapery tail whip his legs. He'd been spotted, and hurriedly swam toward the gate, only to be bumped in the small of his back and pushed face-first into the pool wall. He started to black out but held himself together, feeling the shark whoosh past. Bumping was how sharks tasted their prey. Move, he told himself, pulling himself along the wall until he found the steel gate. He frantically sprang the metal catches.

The water swirled violently around him. They were coming—both of them—he could sense it, and he opened the trap and swam through. With his foot, he slammed the trap shut, heard a loud collision. One of the sharks had wedged its nose into the trap, preventing Hardare from closing it completely. Reaching into his swim trunks, Hardare removed the steel shim and plunged it into the tip of the shark's nose.

The shark backed off. An underwater tunnel had been dug into the end of the pool to let him leave invisibly, and he plunged into it and swam hard, his back burning, his eyes losing their focus. At the tunnel's end he glimpsed a flashing yellow light, and thought how happy he was going to be to hear Frank Stanley curse him out.

"Vince, you goddamned bastard. You're alive." Dropping his flashlight, Frank Stanley kissed him like a long lost son. "Oh, sweet Jesus, I thought you were gone. Vince." He grabbed a metal folding chair and tried to make him sit. "You're shaking like a leaf. Sit down."

"No, I'm okay," Hardare said, trying to get his legs to hold him up straight.

"No, you're not. I'm getting you out of here."

They were behind a tent, and he heard the crowd's

shouting. They thought he was dead. How did he want them to learn he was alive? By reading it in the papers tomorrow? He had to finish the escape, make the payoff.

Frank Stanley held up his robe. "There's an ambulance out front. Where the hell are you going?"

"Got to finish this."

He walked feebly around the tent without being noticed. With a superhuman effort he shoved through a mob of reporters and staggered onto the lawn in front of the blackened pool. A dead shark's carcass floated belly-up. Turning, he faced the hotel, raised his arm, saw their collective expressions.

There was euphoric whooping and yells. Guests leaned over the balconies, cheering. The roar grew. Hardare stood in the center of it, feeling the ovation shake his soul. In their faces he saw happiness, astonishment, in one or two even love. He was a hero. Had he said, "Let's take over City Hall," half of them would have followed him blindly. Death had been cheated. There was no greater cause for rejoicing.

Finally the cheers died and he began to falter. Hotel security men circled around him as Frank Stanley threw a robe over his shoulders. They wedged through the swelling crowd, and with each step his legs grew heavier. He stopped and decided to lie down in the grass.

"Come on Vince, you can do it," Frank Stanley encouraged. "Just a couple more steps. Lean against me."

Reporters swarmed around them, asking a barrage of asinine questions, and his agent swatted away an errant microphone. Someone said, "Hardare, tell our viewers how you feel."

"Great," he managed to whisper.

"Did the shark actually bite you?"

"No," Frank Stanley snapped, "he bit the fucking shark. Piss off."

They reached the hotel's double glass doors and Hardare looked back. Michael Cribbins and another assistant were drawing the gimmicked steel gate up from the pool and would soon replace it with a second, normal gate in case a curious spectator or reporter wanted to inspect it. He smiled weakly, knowing the secret of his escape was safe.

They entered the lobby. His agent said, "Don't fade out on me, Vince. Oh, God, he's going under. Somebody help me."

"Wake me when the scary part's over," Hardare said, crumpling to the floor.

Chapter 9

West End

*J*an Black had only visited London once before, and she had found it an odd coincidence that both trips would bring her to the fashionable section known as the West End. As she got out of the cab, she wondered if remembering that first trip so vividly now was a bad omen, and then just as quickly erased the thought from her mind. During her last trip, her appointment in the West End had come very close to killing her.

Number 87 was a stately Victorian townhouse, and Jan pressed the front buzzer forcefully. Brushing an errant lock of red hair from her face, she appraised her reflection in the glass of the door. Black Spandex miniskirt, black stockings, a purple dashiki, and red pumps: a perfect blend of punkish London chic. She was pressing the buzzer again when the door swung open, and a barefoot man in jeans and a threadbare flannel shirt said, "You got me out of the shower, so this had better be good."

It was *him*. Jan Black stiffened, unable to take her eyes away from his face. He was better looking than on television, his eyes softer, more appealing, or would have been if he wasn't scowling at her. *Stop acting like a teenager*, she told herself: *I am here to do a job, and nothing else*.

"I don't know if you remember me," she said. "My name is Jan Black. We met about a year ago."

"I'd be surprised if I didn't remember you."

She blushed, feeling him soften. "It was at a show at the Magic Circle in Los Angeles. You needed an assistant, and I helped you with the Chinese ring trick."

"Oh." He stared blankly at her. Her face wasn't even vaguely familiar, and Hardare wondered if forgetting spectacular young women was a sign of growing old. He decided to use a line that had gotten him out of trouble before, and said, "You've changed your hair since then."

"That's right." Jan smiled brightly. "I cut it short." A cold draft swept through the doorway. "Do you mind if I come in? It's absolutely bitter out here."

She attempted to step into the warm foyer and Hardare just as adroitly blocked her way. "Perhaps you can first tell me what it is you want."

"I want to talk to you," she said.

"Why?"

"I write features for the Scripps-Howard newspaper syndicate," she explained. "Mostly personality profiles for our Sunday magazine section. I was writing a story on your career."

So that was the hitch. It had been two days since the shark escape, and he'd been purposely avoiding reporters, and had even gone so far as to have his phone number changed. "I'm sorry Ms. Black, but no interviews. I gave a press conference yesterday and said everything that needed to be said." He started to shut the door. "I'm sure you understand."

A wall of resolution rose in her face. She placed her open palm against the door. "Please. It won't take more than fifteen minutes. Then I'll be gone."

"Maybe some other time."

"My newspaper is willing to pay you for an exclusive interview," she said, growing insistant.

"No, thank you."

"They are willing to pay you twenty thousand dollars."

He hesitated. He had a flight out this afternoon to meet Kincaid at his ranch in Brownsville, and could certainly use another twenty thousand to cover expenses. Except that Kincaid had called him the night before to tell him that if he saw Hardare's name one more time in the newspapers, he was backing out of the rescue.

"No," Hardare told her. "Good-bye."

In the kitchen he heard the phone. That had to be his travel agent confirming his reservation and seat assignment. He started to close the door and Jan stuck her foot in. "Look," she said. "Just give me one good quote and I'll leave you alone. That's all I'm asking for. Please."

The phone continued to ring. Hardare contemplated throwing her out, imagined the lawsuit that would ensue, and instead wagged a finger in Jan's face. "Stay here. I'll be right back."

When he returned a minute later she was gone. Infuriated, he followed the arresting scent of her perfume through the living room, then down the narrow hallway. "Hello? Are you still here? Or is your fragrance just haunting me?"

He heard laughter. "In here," she called from the end of the hall. His magic studio, the one room that always fascinated his guests. Cluttered with rare books, blueprints, and mysterious-looking props painted in Chinese restaurant colors, the walls were decorated with original vaudeville posters of his father, Houdini, T. Nelson Downs, The King of Coins, Thurston doing his famous Asrah levitation, and the Indian wizard Sorcar. "I really like this one," she remarked as he came in, pointing to a poster of Hardare suspended by his ankles above a huge crowd. It was an advertisement for British Government Premium Bonds, and the caption beneath it read, *The More Bonds I Have the Happier I am. V. Hardare.* "Do you do a lot of endorsements?" she asked.

He refused to make conversation with her. "If you don't mind, I have to ask you to leave."

She pretended not to hear him, floating around the studio. He saw the direction she was headed in, and before he could intercept her, her hand entered the open suitcase he'd left on a chair. "Are you going on vacation?" she asked, holding up his airline ticket. "Maybe

128

we can share a taxi to the airport, and you can give me an interview."

He snatched the ticket out of her hand before she had a chance to open it. She was looking for something, and it occurred to him that he'd left too many things around the apartment that might make her suspicious, including aerial photographs of Santa Maria prison that Kincaid had sent and his own outline for the escape. If she even got the faintest suspicion of what he was doing, everything he had worked so hard for was ruined.

"It's none of your business, but I'm going to attend a magician's convention in Cleveland. I'm being given an award."

"A magician's convention in Cleveland?" she said skeptically.

"Magic conventions are usually held in obscure places. To keep them secret. I've been asked to perform, and will premiere a brand-new illusion." He paused, sensing that she wasn't buying it, and pointed at a thin wooden board lying between two folding metal chairs in the center of the room. "That's it right there. Took years to design."

"And what am I looking at?" she said, casually inspecting the apparatus. "Or is that a secret too?"

"Not at all. I'll give you a demonstration." He tapped the board with his fingers. "Just sit right here. Don't worry. I didn't embarrass you at the Magic Circle, did I?" She gave him a sideways glance, then sat on the board. "Bring your feet up. Okay, lie down. Keep your back flat. Perfect."

Jan stared up at the ceiling. "I've never done anything like this before."

"Neither have I."

"What?"

"Just kidding. Don't laugh, this is serious business. Lie still." He lifted his arms and spread his fingers wide apart. "One . . . two . . . three. There we go."

Before Jan knew what was happening, she was rising in the air on the thin board. Goosebumps rose on her arms at the same time, and as the board rose past the top of Hardare's head, she glanced into a mirror on the wall. There were no hydraulic poles holding her up, no wires hanging from the ceiling, and she continued to rise and was soon inches from the ceiling.

"That looks fantastic," he said, busily picking up the aerial photographs and notes, stuffing them into the suitcase, and locking it.

"Wonderful," she replied, fidgeting nervously. "Would you mind bringing me down? This isn't fun anymore."

"I thought you said you liked magic," Hardare said.

"Not this much," she muttered, and trying to slide off the board, felt it sway precariously. "Damn," she said as her purse slipped from her fingers and went crashing to the floor below.

The purse hit the chair and spilled open, and Hardare knelt down to retrieve the coins and other loose objects that scattered at his feet. Dropping the coins into the purse, he noticed a spiral pocket notebook with his name written on it. He looked up at Jan. Her head was turned sideways, her radiant green eyes staring at him through the large practice mirror on the wall.

"Please don't be angry," she said.

"Do I have any other choice?" He removed the notepad and scowled. Written on the first page were his name, his address, and his new unlisted phone number.

"How in Christ's name did you get this?" he asked with real anger in his voice. "I got a new unlisted phone number *less than two days ago!*"

"Look, I can explain everything, Mr. Hardare . . ."

"Don't even try," Hardare said, sensing that something was very wrong. He waved his arms mysteriously and the board went up another two inches, pinning her to the ceiling.

"What are you doing?" Jan said breathlessly, barely able to move. "Let me down!"

"When I'm good and ready," Hardare said. He went into the adjacent bedroom, taking her purse with him.

He dumped the purse's contents onto the bed and went through her personal belongings. She seemed to be carrying the barest essentials—one lipstick, a small vanity, breath mints—and he found the photo compartment of her wallet to be completely empty. She was not carrying any identification or press credentials. In a zippered compartment he found the receipts for the clothes she was wearing.

Who was she? Obviously not a reporter.

Taking a suitcase from the closet, Hardare quickly packed the rest of the things he would need for Brownsville. In the other room he could hear Jan repeatedly calling out his name.

Five minutes later he returned to his studio. "Just shut up and listen," Hardare said as Jan tried to speak. "I don't know who you are, and I don't particularly care. I'm going to be leaving in another few minutes, but I have called a magician friend of mine to come over and let you down once I'm gone."

She tried to protest. "But I—"

"Don't waste your breath," Hardare said flatly. "I don't have the time for it."

Then he disappeared into the hallway. Jan felt absolutely ridiculous, and again called out his name. How had she managed to let Hardare put her in such a compromising position, especially with her background and training? She had been so close to getting him to talk, and the next thing she knew, she was floating on the ceiling. Compared to the shark escape, she supposed he would probably consider this a minor distraction.

"Mr. Hardare, if you'd just give me a minute, I can explain everything." A stero came on in another room, and the sounds of a Dixieland jazz band completely enveloped the apartment. Then she heard the front door slam.

Twenty minutes after Hardare had left the West End, a limousine appeared at the end of the block, and slowly edged up to where a black van was parked beside an open manhole cover. Stepping out of the limousine, Richard Lyons tapped twice on the van's side door with his gloved hand. The door slid open, and as Lyons climbed into the van, his limousine quietly drove away.

The van's interior was loaded with sophisticated surveillance equipment and reel-to-reel tape machines. Logan and Dorsey had been monitoring Hardare's phone calls since he had first visited the American Embassy, and had allowed Lyons to keep tabs on the unpredictable magician's comings and goings.

"What have you got for me?" Lyons asked, watching as Logan finished rewinding a tape. Logan pushed a button and let the conversation start to play. The voices were muted and barely intelligible.

"It sounds better over the headsets," Logan said. He picked up a pad and read from his notes. "Hardare has got a Pan American flight to Kennedy at one o'clock, and then a connecting flight to Brownsville that should get him in by eight tonight their time."

"I want you to be at there when he steps off that plane," Lyons said. Dorsey, who was sitting up front watching the street, looked at him through the rearview mirror. "Take the goddamned Concorde if you have to. Just make sure you're there. Frank Kincaid is a blackmailing son-of-a-bitch. I want you watching both him and Hardare as closely as possible. I'll follow you in tomorrow afternoon."

"Whatever you say," was Logan's reply.

As Lyons got out of the van, Dorsey rolled down his window and said to him, "Just before Hardare left, he called a friend and asked him to come over to get a girl down from the ceiling."

Standing on the curb, Lyons scowled at him. "Is this your idea of a joke?"

"We've got it on tape," Dorsey said defensively. His face reddened. "Hardare let a good-looking woman into his apartment twenty minutes ago, but we didn't see her leave."

"Any idea who she is?" Lyons asked.

"We thought you might know," Dorsey said.

Lyons opened his mouth, said nothing. The implication stung, but he supposed he deserved it. Looking across the street at Hardare's townhouse, he said, "Whoever she is, she's not one of ours. I would never send someone in without telling you."

"Maybe we should find out," Dorsey said.

"I think that's a very good idea."

Dorsey got out of the truck, and handed Lyons a navy blue denim jacket identical to the one he was wearing. Then he took a clipboard from the front seat and said, "I wonder how long it's been since someone read their meter?"

Alongside the townhouse was an alley barely wide enough for a man to walk through. Dorsey went first, indicating he wanted to enter through a rear first-floor window. Lyons hung close behind, shielding his partner's illicit actions from the street. Dorsey sprayed a pane of glass in the window with a plastic adhesive, waited ten seconds for it to turn white and dry, then took a small tack hammer from his inner jacket pocket. As Dorsey raised his arm Lyons suddenly whispered, "*Look*. She's right up *there*."

Dorsey looked. And looked. There was a woman lying on a board who appeared to be *stuck* to the ceiling. That could be the only explanation, because from where he was standing the board did not appear to have any visible form of support.

The floating girl did not look like the average floating girl, especially with her red pumps dangling over the end of the board. She appeared to be gradually inching her way down to one end, and had curled her legs in so as not to throw too much weight over the side. It was slow going, and afforded both men several minutes to stare at the underside of the apparatus.

"Can't see how it works," Lyons finally conceded. "At least not from this angle."

"I'd like to examine the board," Dorsey said. Then he added, "Think of the mess we'd have on our hands if he'd cut her in half and left her."

"She's going to jump," Lyons said, watching her kick off her pumps one at a time.

And she did, finally, after several seconds hesitation, and landed on the floor in a crouch. The board quivered noticeably but did not come down. Unfazed, the girl stood, smoothed out her clothes, then found a chair, and pulling it beneath the floating board, climbed up. She craned her neck, looking at the board as closely as possible, yet never actually touching it, as if this was a promise she had made to herself.

"Aha," she unexpectedly said aloud. "Now I understand!"

And with that, she jumped down, slipped on her pumps, and walked out of the room. They heard the front door slam, but they did not move, neither man understanding.

"I'd like to know what the hell she saw," Dorsey muttered.

"So would I," Lyons replied, his face pressed against the frosted pane of glass.

Chapter 10

Second Sight

*A*t approximately the same time that her father was boarding an airplane at Heathrow Airport, Crystal was beginning a new day in Santa Maria prison.

It started with a siren, loud, ear-shattering, right outside her cell window. Then the ghoulish howls that accompanied it like a chorus, the Dobermans penned in the yard crying to get loose. The first morning she'd heard them, she'd burst into tears. *Someone's being tortured to death*, she had thought.

Today was her sixth day, and she no longer awoke

in a state of fear. Easing onto the lidless toilet in her cell, she let her eyes adjust to the darkness. The cell was a closet, barely big enough to hold the three cots, three footlockers, and three women who shared it. Each morning it looked a little smaller, as if during the night someone had pushed in the walls. *Moe, Larry, we're trapped like rats!* she thought, remembering a favorite Three Stooges episode. "Speak for yourself," Moe said with scorn, bonking hapless Curly over the head with a giant pipe. She smiled as she tugged the overhead chain.

Crystal washed as her cellmates stirred. Jennifer was up first. She sat completely naked on the toilet and sang Mr. Rogers' "It's a Beautiful Day in the Neighborhood." Tall, brown-haired, and kindly, Jennifer was the only decent thing Crystal had found inside the prison. Before her arrest for buying coke, she had sung country and western music in a band, and had been good enough to audition for a recording outfit in Nashville. She had been a prisoner for five years; her band had found a new lead, and regularly sent her postcards from places they were playing.

"All you need is an audience," Crystal said when Jennifer was finished.

"Honey, I've already got one of those." Standing, Jennifer flushed the toilet and put her hand to her ear. "Can't you hear that roar of applause? Boy, that girl can sing!"

There was a pitiful moan as their third cellmate came out of her slumber. Mercedes Pareda was a fat, tattooed hooker from Mexico City who had murdered one of her customers. She was also a junkie, although Crystal had no idea who she bought her drugs from. Better not to know, she had decided.

They dressed quickly, artfully avoiding each other in the tiny room. Crystal was ready in five minutes, a feat she would have claimed impossible a week ago at school. She stood at the cell door, and soon Jennifer and Mercedes joined her. They waited.

At 6:55, four guards armed with shotguns entered the cellblock. They unlocked the five cells and ordered the fifteen women inmates out. After a quick head count, they led them down a hall and two flights of stairs, and outside across the courtyard to the mess hall.

Breakfast was served Army-style to three hundred women at once, and Crystal got a tray and stood in a long line. It inched ahead. Behind the counter a pretty woman who was slopping oatmeal reminded Crystal vividly of her mother.

"Anything decent on the menu?" Crystal asked pleasantly.

"Same crummy fucking shit," the woman replied.

She filled her tray with a bowl of oatmeal, day-old bread, a cup of bitter *cafecito*, and a watery glass of Tang. She found a spot at a long table and dug in.

Breakfast was over at 7:20. Under the guards' watchful eyes, the prisoners at each table stood in rotation and marched outside. Crystal was one of the last ones out, hearing again the vulgar hoots from the mob of male inmates waiting in the yard. The ladies responded in kind, making obscene gestures or wiggling their asses suggestively. Standing on tiptoe in back, Crystal felt a finger dig sharply into her back. She turned, facing a stone-faced Maria Alvarez. Maria had been moved onto another floor two days before, and they had not had a chance to talk in private since.

"Hey," Crystal said, "you scared me."

"Turn around. Don't look at me when I speak."
Crystal did as told, and Maria said, "I have a present
for you."

"Huh?"

"Stand still."

Crystal looked away and felt Maria slip what felt
like a folded piece of paper into the back pocket of her
blue jeans.

"What is it?" Crystal whispered nervously.

"Mail from home."

A whistle blew. Protected by an escort of guards,
the warden entered the yard and was handed a cordless
microphone. A broad-chested man with black hair, he
wore a sharkskin suit with wide lapels and shiny black
buttons. "Look at this flaming bozo," a big lesbian said
quite loudly. "Why doesn't he tell jokes? Hear the one
about the Mexican diet? Eat one meal, lose ten pounds."

Laughter, then more whistles. Crystal glanced over
her shoulder; Maria was gone. What did she mean "mail
from home?"

The Mexican flag was raised while the warden attempted to sing the national anthem. Toward the end
his voice faded, and Crystal heard an inmate defiantly
whistling the "Star-Spangled Banner."

The anthem ended. It was nearly 7:40, time for
work. The inmates filed out of the yard, and Crystal
entered Building *A* and walked to the basket shop unes-
corted. Finding her seat at a table cluttered with tools
and dried cane reed, she picked up a basket and examined her previous day's work. The basket was
lopsided—the work of a dreamer. If a basket was im-
perfect she wouldn't get paid, and without money, she

couldn't buy toothpaste, or soap, or candy bars from the prison store. She dejectedly pulled it apart.

Measuring a strip of reed, she cut it, and started to weave according to a pattern thumbtacked to the wall. It was absorbing work and usually let her forget where she was. After five minutes she walked up to the front of the shop and said to the guard on duty, "I have to take a pee."

The guard tapped the face of his wristwatch. "Five minutes," he said.

Crystal hurried down the hallway toward the restrooms. Going inside, she quickly checked the five doorless stalls, found them empty, and sat down on the end toilet. You learn something everywhere you go, her father had often said when they were traveling. In prison Crystal had learned to be careful.

She dug the piece of paper out of her pants pocket. It was a tightly folded sheet of newspaper, and she carefully opened it on the lid of the toilet. It was from a three-day-old copy of *USA TODAY*, and the vivid four-color photographs covering both sides of the page at first did not look real.

Crystal heard herself gasp. It was a feature article about her father. She stared at the montage of photographs, realizing they were in sequence, and designed to let the reader see exactly what had occurred in Blackpool, England, a few days before.

In the first photograph, her father was dressed in an ugly blue bathing suit and standing with a mob of TV people. Behind him was a huge rectangular swimming pool with cobalt blue water.

In the next photograph her father was inside a packing case, and being lowered into the pool. Then a steel gate leading to another pool was lifted, and three dangerous-looking sharks swam into the picture. Crystal bit her lip at the sight of them. "The Jaws of Death."

Three years ago her father had dreamed up the idea, and had been successful selling it to a hotel in Vegas and the executives of one of the TV networks, but not to her mother. They had practically had a divorce over it one night at the dinner table. It would be the most spectacular escape of his career, he'd argued for over an hour. Bigger than anything his dad, or Houdini, had ever done. "Not while I'm alive," her mother had said repeatedly, not once touching her food. "I couldn't watch you being eaten alive."

In the next series of photographs it appeared that the sharks had gone crazy, heaving themselves across the pool, people screaming, blood darkening the water; Crystal shook her head. Her mom had always known what was best.

The sharks were creating a bloodbath. In the next shot she saw her father's head had come up, gasping for air. A shark had crept up behind him. "Look out," she said without thinking. The shark bit her father in the chest while the crowd roared. His head disappeared beneath the water. A tear dribbled down Crystal's cheek.

She turned the newspaper over on the lid. Out of nowhere her father had appeared at poolside, looking exhausted but still very much alive. He held up his clenched fist and the crowd erupted. How had he survived? Coming up for air wasn't part of the trick. Something had gone wrong, nearly killed him.

She flipped the page back over, found the beginning of the story, and started reading. After her mother had died, she'd never thought her father would ever again try a truly dangerous escape. The one time he'd really needed to pull off a miracle, he hadn't pulled through. It had hurt him terribly, still hurt him now. And it had forever changed the way she saw him.

But then, reading the story, all the old feelings swept over her. The shark escape had created a minor sensation. It was estimated that over ten million people worldwide had watched it on cable TV. Once again people were labeling him the world's greatest escape artist. It had to mean so much to him. She started to cry and found she could not stop.

The bathroom door slammed open. "Your five minutes are up!" roared the guard from the shop.

She swallowed a huge gulp. Inmates were not allowed to have newspapers. And if the guard searched her and found it, which was possible, she was permanently screwed. She wiped away the last of her tears, brought the folded newspaper up to her lips, and kissed her father's picture. Then she shredded the article into small pieces, lifted the toilet lid, and flushed them away.

Work stopped at noon. Lunch was served in the yard, pork and refried beans the main fare. Crystal had gone back to work feeling a strange elation, and proceeded to finish a nearly perfect basket. She was sitting in the cool shade of a building still feeling good about it when Maria sat down beside her.

"Thanks for the mail," Crystal said. Maria nodded

and started to eat. "How did you get hold of a news-paper?"

"Bribed a guard," Maria replied, still chewing.

"You gave him money? Where did you get it?"

"I gave him a blowjob," Maria said, and when she saw Crystal staring at her, glared back. "I didn't have much choice."

"What are you talking about?" Crystal said indignantly. "What's so important about a newspaper? What would you have done if he had offered to buy you a steak dinner?"

Maria stopped eating and angrily threw her fork onto the tin plate. "You little bitch," she hissed in Spanish, and pulling off her sneaker, removed a tiny sliver of paper and unrolled it like a scroll in front of Crystal's eyes. It was the listing from a classified section of a newspaper and it read, *Maria, All is not lost! We think of you always and look forward—soon, we hope—to the day when we can be together again. Write if you can. Love, Sam & the boys*

When she saw Crystal had finished, she rolled the tiny paper back up. Maria's anger had faded and she said, "The people I work for use the classifieds to communicate with agents who are on the run or in prison."

"The people you work for? What are you, some kind of spy?"

"It's a very long story, Crystal."

"Hey, I've got plenty of time."

Maria laughed faintly. She looked around carefully before speaking. "I am a field agent for the CIA, mostly undercover. Eighteen months ago, your Drug Enforcement Agency asked us to cooperate in an operation to stop the enormous flow of drugs coming out of Mexico

144

into the States. My job was to gather names and pass them along. Guerra is one of those most heavily involved."

"Does Guerra deal?"

"He deals, he supplies, he smuggles. He started two years ago, when he busted a coke dealer. The guy offered him half his business if Guerra would drop charges. Guerra agreed, spent six months learning the ropes, then had the dealer killed. He's absorbed a lot of other drug operations that way."

"Great guy."

"He's the most influential drug lord in the country. Everyone is in his pocket, or was. And the officials and police he can't bribe aren't about to stop him, because he's one of their own."

"He's probably got great dirt on them," Crystal said.

"But now," Maria went on, "he's in trouble. His empire is crumbling. Many of his associates are in jail or gone into hiding. Soon he'll join them, you wait." Her eyes briefly met Crystal's. "You and I are his insurance right now. When he's finally caught, he'll offer us as a trade. That's why he's gone to such elaborate measures to be sure no one can rescue us."

Crystal thought a moment. "That message," she said. "From the paper. Do you know what it means?"

"Yes." Maria said quietly. "They want me to communicate with them, if possible. They also want me to know that they are working to gain our freedom."

"Do you believe them?" Crystal asked.

"Of course," Maria said. "If they couldn't help us, they would say so. The newspaper was worth what I paid. It has given me hope again." Maria leaned straight back against the wall of the concrete building and drew her knees up beneath her chin. "I have lost practically everything else," she went on. "My father, my little brother, whom I raised, my lover Miguel. Lost them all, forever. But I still have hope. I hope for the day that I can walk out of here, and destroy the man who murdered them." Maria's eyes were glistening and she wiped them dry. "It is all I seem . . . to have left."

The words choked her. Crystal touched Maria's wrist and said, "Why did Guerra murder your father?"

"After my little brother was murdered, my father lost interest in life, and locked himself up in his house. He died a few months later in his sleep." Maria suddenly regained her composure herself. Picking up her plate, she found her appetite and started eating. "Talking about it will only get me very depressed. So let's not talk about it anymore, all right?"

Crystal watched her eat. When Maria was finished, Crystal said, "If you got out, could you really destroy Guerra?"

"I—" Maria hesitated, then got to her feet, brushing the red dirt from her jeans. "I'll talk to you later."

"Maybe I can help you," Crystal offered, and watched her walk briskly away.

The rest of the day passed uneventfully. Crystal went back to work, then to dinner, searching the crowded mess hall, hoping to find Maria. She didn't see the woman's pretty face. She looked again; no Maria. The meal was gray soup and boiled vegetables. Crystal sipped at it, then tried to figure out what it was. She glanced across the hall, and saw Maria sitting at the end of a long table by herself.

"Can you do it, or not?" Crystal asked, startling Maria as she sat down beside her.

Maria looked at her quizzically. "Can I do what?"

Whispering, Crystal said, "Destroy Guerra?"

"That is none of your business," she replied, and immediately started to get up from the table.

Crystal slapped her hand on Maria's arm. "Hey! You got me involved in this mess. I have a right to know. Tell me."

Maria sat back down, and in an angry whisper said, "I can destroy his operation. I suppose that is as good as destroying him. I know enough to shut him down. If—"

"Then why don't you?" Crystal interrupted. "There's a Mexican woman in Building *B* who can get letters smuggled out. My friend Jennifer knows her. Why not send your people a note and give them this information? If Guerra gets arrested, then it stands to reason you and I will get released from here, doesn't it?"

"I know all about the woman in Building *B*," Maria replied, her face growing flush. "Her name is Contessa, and she has an arrangement with one of the head guards. However, I also know that this guard personally reads every letter that goes out. If he even became remotely suspicious, he'd destroy the letter."

"Why not send it in code?" Crystal said. "Then he won't know what it means."

A pained expression crossed Maria's face. "That also occurred to me. Unfortunately, the people I work for were anxious to get me on the street when I first offered my services, and the actual training I received lasted less than a month. I never learned how to send or receive codes." She offered Crystal a sad smile. "Your idea is a good one. I, unfortunately, am not good enough to carry it out."

Crystal hesitated. "Are your people good at cracking codes?"

"Of course. Why?"

"Because I know one that my father developed."

Maria suddenly sat up very straight at the table. "Who knows the code besides you, and your father?"

"My mother used to know it, but she's dead now."

"Did your father develop it himself?"

"He sort of adopted it from one used by the Zancigs," Crystal said. "They were a nightclub act. They called themselves 'Two Minds that Think as One.' My father liked their code because it used normal words, odd sounds, and also voice inflection."

"So this was something you and your father did on stage?"

"That's right. The act was called 'Second Sight.' I was actually pretty good at it."

Maria's eyes widened, and for the first time since Crystal had known her, her entire face broke into a smile. Pinching Crystal's arm, she said, "I want to know more. How it works, how you learned it. Please. Tell me everything."

"Okay," Crystal said.

Learning "Second Sight" had actually been her mother's idea.

Crystal was then eight, and acutely shy. When

148

strangers had visited their apartment in New York she had often run upstairs, or hidden behind the couch. She rarely looked people in the eye when spoken to. To make matters worse, she missed her father terribly. He was away for weeks and sometimes months at a time, doing shows in Las Vegas and appearing on television. One night, as he was introduced on the Johnny Carson show, she saw him walk out wearing a newly grown mustache, and she had not immediately recognized him. She had burst into tears.

The next day her mother had an idea. Years before, when she and Vincent were dating, he had taught her a secret language used by vaudeville psychics called "Second Sight." From then on, they had used the secret language constantly, in letters, over the phone, even on stage when they wanted to talk secretly. If Crystal learned "Second Sight," her mother guaranteed her that her father would spend more time with her.

After a few weeks, Crystal had learned the alphabet and the numbers one through ten. At her mother's urging, she wrote her father a letter in code, wishing him a happy birthday and asking him to come home soon. The day he received it, he called her from Paris. They had spent over an hour on the phone.

When he came home weeks later, he and Crystal had spent every evening expanding their vocabulary. "Second Sight," he had explained, was usually performed by a husband-and-wife team. The wife, posing as the psychic, would sit on stage blindfolded while her smooth-talking husband would roam through the audience and ask his wife to identify articles that spectators held in their hands, or repeat remarks whispered into the husband's ear. But there was no reason why Crystal couldn't play the psychic. In fact, he decided, it might give a breath of fresh air to the routine.

They had practiced constantly. Her father would stand on one side of the living room, hold up his clenched fist, and say, "I want you to think hard, please . . . Be quick."

After some hesitation Crystal would answer, "You are holding a coin in your hand. A quarter. The date is 1965."

If she was right, the article in his hand, usually a coin or a dollar bill, became hers. Working with money was good training, since it forced her to decipher several code words at once in order to learn the date on the coin or bill. To make it a little easier for her, her father had modified the code words for the numbers one through ten. Because each word had the same number of letters as the number it represented, this part of the code was almost impossible to forget.

> "I" stood for the number *1*.
> "Am" stood for the number *2*.
> "Can" stood for the number *3*.
> "Wait" stood for the number *4*.
> "Quick" stood for the number *5*.
> "Please" stood for the number *6*.
> "Crystal" stood for the number *7*.
> "All right" stood for the number *8*.
> "Think hard" stood for the number *9*.
> "Oh" stood for *zero*.

After weeks of practice, they began to perform "Second Sight" for neighbors and visiting relatives. Soon, at her insistance, they expanded the code. Crystal was afraid that if anyone saw the routine a few times, the code would become obvious. After some experimentation, her father came up with a new wrinkle. He would hold several articles in his hand at a time. This meant additional talking on his part, but the code was now so routine it didn't matter. They tried the "new" trick out, and to their amazement, found it baffled everyone who saw it, including many of her father's well-posted magic friends.

Within a few months Crystal's total vocabulary had reached over two hundred words. She could now identify any object found in the home, or on someone's person. The summer was approaching, and her father was booked to appear at the Moulin Rouge in Paris. Crystal had dreaded his leaving, especially with school out and nothing for her to do. The morning of his flight he had kissed them good-bye, and gone downstairs to take a taxi to Kennedy Airport. Teary-eyed, Crystal went to her room, and found a packed suitcase on her bed, an airplane ticket on top. For a moment she had thought she was dreaming, then let out an elated yell. She had dragged the suitcase into the hall, and found her mother standing there, luggage in hand. They had taken the elevator downstairs and gotten into the taxi her father had waiting for them at curbside.

Their act had caused a minor sensation with the noisy Parisian crowds. Crystal was billed as a child psychic—"*She sees into the mind!*"—and their booking was extended through the end of the summer. To further confound their audiences, her father added another twist. Before he spoke to Crystal, he would ask a spectator to concentrate on the object he was holding. This request was done in code, and gave Crystal the information she needed. When her father did address her, he simply said "Crystal?" and, after a slight pause, she would reveal the item, without any apparent prompting by her father.

She had spent ten weeks in Paris with her mother and father, working, playing, being a family. She still remembered it as the happiest time of her entire life.

By the time Crystal was finished explaining "Second Sight," Maria was breathless. "If you put your code in a letter," she said, "could you make it simple enough for my people to break?"

"Of course," Crystal said. "My father's code isn't difficult at all. What made the act work was our timing and delivery. I don't think it would take your people very long to learn it."

Maria could not contain herself. She leaned forward so she was breathing in Crystal's face and said, "In two days a Delta Airlines 747 will be flying from Mexico City to Los Angeles with over a thousand pounds of heroin hidden in its hold. How would you like to help me stop that plane from ever taking off?"

"And win a medal from Nancy Reagan? Sure, why not?"

Maria grabbed Crystal by the shoulders and kissed her. "You are a godsend," Maria told her.

Chapter 11

Brownsville

Kincaid met Hardare in the baggage claim area of Brownsville International Airport, his camouflage fatigue pants, black turtleneck sweater, and ten-gallon black Stetson hat looking no more out of place than the chubby Mexican woman with a basket of live chickens or the barefoot family of eleven that had come to greet their father. They shook hands, and beneath Kincaid's arm Hardare spied a rolled-up copy of the current issue of *Newsweek*.

"Sign many autographs on the plane?" Kincaid asked him.

Hardare had read the same issue on the flight, including the nice blurb and picture about his shark escape in the "People" section. "I kept my face buried in a book," he replied, seeing his two suitcases miraculously appear together on the carousel.

"Good." Taking the heavier suitcase, Kincaid led him outside to the parking lot. "In my work, you have to maintain a low profile if you want to stay in business and stay alive."

"You don't have to apologize," Hardare said, "I understand your need for secrecy. After all, we are breaking the law."

They crossed the lot, and then Kincaid introduced Hardare to "The Fuhrer's Pride," a souped-up black Volkswagen bus with mag wheels and a new six-cylinder engine. They piled into the front seat and Kincaid fired up the engine, then drove out of the parking lot at what seemed like a hundred miles an hour. It was nearly dusk; a sliver of orange sun flickered on the pale horizon like a dying ember. Clouds of dust swirled around them.

Kincaid turned on his radar detector and entered a major six-lane highway. Watching his mirror he said, "We're being tailed."

Hardare turned around in his seat.

"Blue Chevy Nova, license Z4A-631. A rental. Two gents in their early forties. I spotted them in the parking lot." He shifted into fifth gear. "Let's see if they're any good."

The car was too far back for Hardare to make out

either of the men clearly. "Who do you think they are?" he asked.

"Hard to say," Kincaid answered, blowing by a turbo Porsche. "I've pissed people off all over the world. Sooner or later someone gets up the nerve to pay me back." The highway opened up, and he got a few hundred yards ahead of the Nova, then locked the VW's wheels and spun the steering wheel hard to his left. The VW screeched down the highway, twisting in a wild bootleg turn. They jumped the concrete median and finally came to a stop in the opposing lane, facing the opposite direction. The Nova sped by them.

Hardare let out a whoop. "I'm impressed." He smiled at Kincaid and heard him grumble. Turning, he saw the Nova behind them.

"How the hell . . . ?"

"They're pros," Kincaid explained. "But I don't think they're from around here." He pushed the accelerator to the floor. "These roads are filled with surprises."

Hardare continued watching the Nova as it doggedly followed them, never getting more than five or six cars back. He glanced once at the dashboard, and saw they were exceeding ninety, and sensed that Kincaid was willing to go much faster if he had to.

"Hang on to your teeth," Kincaid said, approaching an exit that appeared to be under construction. The VW hit a wooden sawhorse at eighty and sent it flying over the guard rail. They raced down a curving exit until the macadam vanished and the VW was skidding dangerously across a steep gravel road. Kincaid turned the wheels into the skid, and after a few hairy moments, regained control and braked beside an embankment of rocks.

"Why are you *stopping*?" Hardare asked anxiously.

"Because there ain't no place else to go."

The Nova came down the exit ramp in hot pursuit. Hitting the gravel, it also skidded, but the driver did not react fast enough, and as the rear wheels spun out of control, the rental car disappeared from the road and down a deep pit. They heard it hit bottom with a heavy crunching sound.

"See you boys in the funny papers," Kincaid called out as he sped away.

When they were back on the highway, Hardare said, "Are you just going to leave them?"

"What do you suggest?" Kincaid asked. "Going back and shooting them, or calling the police?"

"Neither. But they were after you."

"Somebody probably hired them," he said, pushing the bus to what Hardare soon realized was his customary breakneck speed. "They were just doing their job."

Kincaid's anti-terrorist training school was located in Olmito, a sleepy town a half-hour's drive north of Brownsville. He drove in through a back entrance and gave Hardare the twenty-five-cent tour. Two hundred acres contained a firing range, a man-made lagoon for boating and demolition courses, a road track, a stucco building that served as a school, his private ranch house, and a small airstrip for his twin-engine Cessna. He had opened the school four years ago to teach anti-terrorist techniques to private corporations, and had never suffered less than a ninety percent occupancy. *"Freedom from fear"* was how he advertised it in the classified sections of *Forbes* and *Fortune* magazines. Peace of mind, for a price.

"If business is so good," Hardare said as they parked at the ranch house, "why do free-lance? For the excitement?"

He laughed contemptuously, slamming his door as he got out. "This business is a scam, and eventually the companies I deal with are going to wise up, and stop shelling out big bucks. Free-lance is what I do best. What's going to keep me going after I shut this place down?"

Hardare helped him get their luggage out of the back. "I would think with the rise in terrorism, your business would be flourishing for years."

"It would—if I was in Europe, or the Middle East. The threat of terrorism in this country is practically non-existent."

"What about American companies abroad?" Hardare said, holding open the front door as Kincaid followed him inside. "Wouldn't they be likely targets?"

"Oh, sure. And they're my biggest clients. We teach them how to avoid having their CEOs kidnapped, how to protect against car bombings, all that crap. And they love to buy the gadgets, you know, the Kevlar vests, bulletproof briefcases and umbrellas, rubber underwear in case they wet their pants. Over fifty million bucks a year is being spent on this garbage." He stopped in the spacious living room and a Mexican houseboy appeared, relieved them of their bags, and silently trudged upstairs. Moments later an aproned woman brought in a tray with two tall iced teas. "Do you have any idea how many Americans were directly affected by terrorism last year?"

Hardare sipped the tangy drink and took a guess. "A thousand?"

"Ninety-four," he said, "and every one made the newspapers. Compare that to the three hundred and seventy-five kids in Detroit that got shot last year, or the two hundred and sixty people murdered in Miami over drugs, and you realize how out of whack the whole situation is."

Kincaid opened a sliding door and they walked out onto a wooden deck. In the distance Hardare could see a firing range, and a lone figure taking practice in the semi-darkness. "This used to be a cattle range," Kincaid said, his right arm making a large definitive sweep. "I suppose in another ten years, when the craze dies down, I'll turn it back into that."

"Sounds like one of your students is having some fun," Hardare said, hearing a pistol being fired so rapidly that he could not count the shots.

"That's an instructor. One of my best." A few moments later the gunfire ended, leaving an eerie stillness once the echoes died. The instructor got into a jeep and floored it, driving across several bumpy hills and directly toward them.

Sipping his drink, Hardare said, "Why does he practice in the dark?"

"She says it makes her rely more on her other senses."

"Your best instructor is a *she*?" Hardare asked.

The jeep braked in front of them and Kincaid said, "That's right. I believe you've already met."

Stepping out of the driver's seat, the instructor removed her oversized black cap, and a torrent of red hair fell to her shoulders. "Good evening, Mr. Hardare," she said.

Hardare stared into the face of Jan Black. "She works for *you*?" he practically shouted, the indignation rising in his voice. "Let me get this straight. You sent her—"

Kincaid did not let him finish. "Jan was in Paris finishing up a consulting job. When I heard about the shark escape, I thought it was a big fake. I asked Jan to pay you a call, and make sure you were really up to rescuing your kid. From what she told me, you're more than ready."

"How would she know?" Hardare replied, still angry. "I didn't tell her a thing."

"You could say he left me hanging," Jan said.

Hardare glared at her. "Who writes your material?"

"Excuse me," she said.

"Whoever it is, fire him," Hardare said. "He's not funny."

Turning to face Kincaid, Hardare said, "You weren't planning to bring her along, were you?"

"Yes, I was," Kincaid replied. "Like I said, she's one of my best. Jan's lived in Mexico, knows the customs and the language. She's also an excellent pilot. She was my first choice to back us up. If you want me to try and find a replacement, I'll be happy to. You're the client, Mr. Hardare."

Hardare struggled with his anger. "I'm not interested in working with people who are second-best." He shot Jan a glance. "If you're that good, I want you on the team."

Jan's lips formed the thinnest smile. "I'll try not to

disappoint you, Mr. Hardare. Frank, Roberto asked me to tell you that he left two sticks of dynamite in the tool box in your bus. I also need to borrow the keys to the storeroom."

Kincaid dug the keys out and tossed them to her. Jan took a step toward the jeep. "Mr. Hardare, after you left I managed to climb down from your floating board. It's a wonderful illusion, but I saw exactly how it works."

"Too bad you had no one to share it with," Hardare said.

Jan started to reply, thought better of it, and hopped into the jeep and sped away. They finished their drinks in silence.

"I did some checking around," Kincaid finally said. "There's a bartender in town named Tanner who did two years in Santa Maria. Said he'd tell us everything he remembered for a hundred bucks. Told me to drop by before he got busy."

Despite his jet lag and lack of sleep, Hardare was anxious to get started. "I'm ready when you are."

When they were out on the highway and doing eighty, Hardare said to Kincaid, "I don't want any more surprises, okay?"

Staring at the road, Kincaid said, "Sure thing."

"Where did you find her, anyway?"

"Jan? Her father was my first commanding officer in Vietnam back in sixty-five. Sergeant Charlie 'Buckeye' Black. When Jan appeared on my doorstep four years ago saying she wanted to become an instructor, I figured

Buck had put her up to it." Kincaid let out a short laugh. "First day here, I put her into an advanced Tae Kwon Do class. She kicked shit for two hours. I put her onto the firing range. Same results. I hired her on the spot. Jan is as complete a soldier as I've ever seen. I guess Buck raised her to be the son he never had."

Ten miles later, Kincaid turned south off U.S. 47 and drove toward Momma's Boys, a ramshackle road-side bar that sprawled along the side of the highway. Built a piece at a time, most of it was covered with a galvanized roof, the rest black tar paper. They parked in the lot, and waited for the dust to settle. In a tool shed behind the bar a man with a ponytail was customizing the engine on a Harley-Davidson with an acetylene torch. Kincaid watched him intently, mumbled some mumbo jumbo about Gary Bang pistons and a Weber carb, and as they got out saw a rabid-looking German shepherd chained to the shed. The beast stretched its neck a full six inches, barking viciously.

Four bikes were parked by the door, and at a glance Kincaid identified them: BMW 972, a GS-series Suzuki, a Laverda, and a Gold Wing Honda. He called them "shovels," bad, burly machines, each a quarter-ton or more. Then he said, "These boys live in a kind of tribal society. They believe in myths and legends, are heavy into drugs, have an unwritten set of laws that everyone understands. You get hard with them, they'll stomp you into the ground. Act soft, they'll do worse."

The screen door slapped shut behind them. An unfinished bar stretched across the back of the room, with a dozen luncheon stools bolted to the floor in front of it. There were several badly stained wooden tables, each big enough for eight chairs around it. Lifesize posters of naked biker playmates, all giant-breasted, with eyes ringed black by mascara, hung behind the bar. The air reeked of sour beer and cigarettes. The King was on the jukebox, wailing.

Four thick, unpleasant-looking, bearded men wearing identical sleeveless tank tops, studded denim vests, and a jungle of blue-black tattooing on their Popeye-sized arms, sat at the bar, guzzling draft beer. As Hardare and Kincaid edged up to the bar, the men stopped horsing around and cussing, and sent their meanest no-nonsense stares down the bar. Kincaid returned the looks, yawned.

"You're that soldier boy," a biker with a scraggly red beard said. "The Vietnam hero. Mr. Stars and Stripes Forever."

"In the flesh," said Kincaid.

"I heard someone say you was a queer. That true, soldier boy? You a dick-sucking, ass-licking mamsy pamsy?"

Kincaid gave him a pause. "How bad you want to find out?"

The brother sitting next to Red Beard choked on his laughter and got a vicious elbow in the ribs for his trouble.

The stick of a man tending bar was not laughing. At least six feet and not more than a hundred and forty pounds, he wore a day-old beard, his sun-bleached hair in flowing locks to his shoulders, his facial expression one of pure hatred. "You march in here looking for trouble, you picked the right fucking place."

"Tanner? I'm Kincaid. We spoke earlier."

"I told you to come early, before the crowd."

"This is crowded? Four fat ladies, me and my partner."

"Jesus fucking Christ, don't start in if you've got half a fucking brain in your fucking head." Tanner tapped two Schlitz drafts, set them on the bar, and Kincaid removed a folded fifty from his breast pocket, and dropped it into a puddle of foam.

"You said a hunnert," he protested. "You said—"

"I haven't seen what you're selling."

Tanner gave him a hardened scowl, lifted a portion of the bar, and took them back into a filthy kitchen. Up on the shelf a radio was blasting an ancient Led Zeppelin song. Tanner yanked the plug out of the wall to turn it off. He cleared a table in the center of the room, and from behind a rattling refrigerator took a rolled sheet of construction paper and laid it out, weighing down the corners with four tomatoes. He had sketched the prison as he remembered it, showing where the guards patrolled, the fences, where the inmates worked, slept, ate their meals, and the numerous guardhouses. The drawing was painstakingly accurate—he'd even included the dog pens—and they spent a minute crouched over it, drawing imaginary paths with their eyes.

"Where'd you learn to draw?" Kincaid asked.

"In the can."

"Santa Maria?"

"Give me a break. Leavenworth. They had a vocational training program. What I got in Santa Maria was dysentery." He took a quart of milk from the Frigidaire. "Lost sixty fucking pounds, most of it brown. Doctor said drinking milk was a safe way to put on weight. Not that I'm apologizing, but I usually have beer."

"Ever see anyone try to escape?" Hardeen asked.

"Couple of tries."

"Anyone make it out alive?"

"One dude beat his rap. Had help from the outside. Old lady waiting in a car."

"Yo, Tanner, you still work here?" a hoarse voice bellowed from the bar. "Things are getting a little faggoty back there. Tell your girlfriends to pull their pants back on. We need another round of brews, Bones."

"Want me to talk to your buddies?" Kincaid inquired.

"Hey, save your jokes for later." He left.

"You hear a funny buzzing?" Kincaid said. He brushed past Hardare and found a door partially hidden behind a pile of boxes in the back of the kitchen. He opened it without making any noise, then silently motioned to Hardare to come over and look. Inside a small windowless room a big-assed girl wearing nothing but a Grateful Dead T-shirt was having a red and purple tattoo emblazoned on her doughy left cheek. Her tattooer, who wore an artist's beret over his gleaming head, seemed hypnotized by the buzzing of his needle machine, and did not hear Kincaid whisper, "He's writing something on her ass. What the hell does it say?"

"Probably 'Enter Here.' "

They heard a glass shatter in the bar. Closing the door, they went back to their spots. Tanner returned, his face and hair dripping beer. He dried himself with a towel and said, "While back, I rode in a gang, got a kick out of busting guys' chops. When a brother got in a wreck, I'd hire a hooker to cocktease him in the hospital. Boys like to pay me back now and then. Bust up the joint."

"What was the interior of the prison like?" Hardare asked, eager to learn as much as he could.

"Outdated. Nothing electronically controlled or fancy like that. Lots of bars and locked doors."

"Did the guards use a master key or work off a ring? Think hard. It's important."

"They used a monster ring of keys. About thirty or more."

"Is that a problem?" Kincaid asked Hardare.

He was interrupted by the sound of a table overturning in the bar. Tanner left, this time taking a towel with him. Kincaid picked up a tomato holding the map, bit into it. "You didn't answer my question."

"Most older prisons have a series of locks, and a few master keys. Santa Maria seems to be an exception. It's probably been built a little bit at a time. All the locks are different. No one single key can open them."

Kincaid finished the tomato. "Or one single lock-pick."

"You've got it."

"How hard does that make it for you?"

"It will be harder."

"But not impossible."

"No. But it won't be a stroll through the woods, either."

Kincaid laughed with his mouth full. "No one said it was."

Tanner returned to the kitchen a different man. Picking up the milk carton, he flung it defiantly across the room. He pointed his finger at a faded snapshot of a flexing musclehead taped above the sink. "That was

165

me, before my body went to hell. Nobody pushed me around, broke up my shit." His hand found a butcher knife in the soapy dishwater. "I'm going to carve my initials in their stomachs. Forget-me-nots."

Kincaid slapped the knife out of his hand as if disciplining a child. Tanner tried to fight, slipped, and landed awkwardly on the seat of his pants. He buried his face in his hands.

"Got to beat it," Kincaid said, rolling up the map. He started to leave and Hardare said, "Give him the other fifty."

Kincaid shoved the bill into the breast pocket of Tanner's workshirt. "We appreciate your help. The information."

"Fuck your mothers," he swore. His eyes had filled with tears, and he looked to the ceiling for help. "God, grant me one stupid wish. Make me strong again. Just for an hour."

The parking lot was pitch dark and Hardare tripped on a beer can before his eyes adjusted to the moonlight. As they approached "The Fuhrer's Pride," Kincaid stopped abruptly, stiffening. The ground around the VW was shimmering, and Kincaid took a flashlight out of the glove compartment and inspected the damage. Someone had broken the rear window on the passenger side, taking off a good deal of paint in the process. Kincaid stalked around the VW, growling like a bear. "At least six hundred in repairs. Could have jimmied the door, but they had to leave a message. 'Fuck you,' this says."

"Anything stolen?"

He climbed through the VW and said, "Yeah, my collection of country and western cassettes."

On the front seat of the VW Hardare found the paperback novel that he had been reading on the plane. The envelope containing the snapshots of Crystal that he was using as a bookmark had been removed, and torn to shreds. Now he could not show Kincaid what his daughter looked like. Hardare picked up the pieces from the floor and put them into his pocket.

"We're going inside to settle this," Kincaid declared. Rolling up his shirtsleeves, he emptied his pockets onto the front seat. "There are three things a man doesn't fuck with—another man's land, his woman, or his wheels. Those are unwritten laws that everyone respects. Or are *made* to respect."

Hitching up his pants, Kincaid sauntered up to the four bikes parked by the front door. Taking a crash helmet adorned with swastikas from the sissy bar, he neatly crushed the taillights on each bike, then lofted the helmet high into the air; it sailed over the toolshed. Lifting his leg, Kincaid kicked the Laverda. The bike toppled over, and in accordance with the domino principle, took the other three bikes down with it. Then he noticed Hardare. "What are you doing?" he demanded.

Hardare had found the toolbox Kincaid kept under the back seat of the VW, and the dynamite. He had broken open both sticks and was pouring the volatile dark powder into small squares of Kleenex and then twisting them into small packets with the ends serving as fuses.

"We're going to do this my way," Hardare told him.

167

When Kincaid did not respond, he said, "You're going to like this."

The soldier of fortune turned silent, and Hardare scrutinized him in the dim light from the bar. Kincaid was six-one and perhaps one hundred ninety pounds, none of it fat. He depended upon his physical prowess to stay alive, that was his business. And who were the four meaty bullies holed up inside? Probably factory workers or car mechanics who smoked pot, drank a six-pack every night, and rode around terrorizing the locals on weekends. It would be a fair fight, except that Hardare had never believed in using his fists. There was a better way, and Hardare was going to show Kincaid what it was.

"You with me or not?" Hardare asked. Kincaid nodded, fell in line behind him. Hardare said, "When we go in, don't let any of them sneak up behind me."

"You're the boss."

The screen door slapped shut behind them. Hardare cleared his throat and the bar went quiet. "I was wondering if any of you saw who broke into my friend's bus and stole his tapes?"

One of the bikers snickered. Red Beard, his beer belly rolling with laughter, said, "Can't say we did."

"That's too bad. Broke into my van and vandalized your bikes. Makes me sick just to think about it."

"Did *what* to our bikes?"

"Vandalized, as in 'vandals.' It's a Latin word. Smashed your taillights and stole Hitler's crash helmet. Then Frank—I mean the vandals—knocked them on the ground in a big heap."

The four bikers jumped off their stools, and Hardare saw Tanner duck into the kitchen. "Mister, you mess with our bikes, it's like screwing our mothers," Red Beard declared, leading the advance. "I've stomped on dudes just for leaning on my Laverda."

Hardare stuck his hands into his pockets, and the human wall stopped. His left hand fingerpalmed four of the explosives, while his right classic-palmed a disposable lighter. One of the bikers drew a knife. Hardare brought his hands out slowly, feigning innocence. "Here's what I'm looking for," Hardare said, pulling a red bandana from his shirt pocket and letting it unfold.

Hardare stroked the bandana mysteriously between his hands. To Red Beard he said, "What's your name?"

"It's Tank, Spermo."

"Tank, would you mind giving my friend back his country and western tapes?"

"Hell, no."

"Your mistake." Hardare stroked the bandana again. A spark appeared in its folds, and by snapping the cloth sharply, he shot the lit explosive across the bar into Red Beard's chest. There was a flash of white and a small explosion. Red Beard flew backwards into one of his friends, and they hit the floor together and did not get up. Dust rose from the floorboards.

"Drop it," Hardare told the knife-wielding biker. The biker hesitated, and Hardare snapped the bandana. A wooden chair beside the biker blew apart. The biker dropped the knife.

"Get out!" Hardare yelled. As the man ran, Hardare pointed at the remaining biker, who wore a black eyepatch, and said, "Where are the tapes?"

"Don't know what you're talking about," he mumbled.

"You think I'm kidding around?" Hardare said,

picking up his friend's pearl-handled switchblade from the floor.

"Be careful with that, Hardare," he heard Kincaid caution.

He threw the knife into his left hand, then his right. The biker's good eye darted from hand to hand. Hardare spread his left fingers wide apart; the knife was gone.

"Huh . . . ?" The biker took a step back.

The knife reappeared in Hardare's right hand. He flicked it into the air, made it invisible again, kept coming forward. The biker retreated another step, then another, and Hardare deftly reproduced the knife out of thin air and flicked the blade beneath the biker's nose. "I can cut your balls off," he said, "And you won't even know it."

"We hid them behind the bar," the biker said, swallowing hard. "Right next to the ice chest. You can have them back."

"Which one of you destroyed my daughter's photographs?"

The biker shut his mouth. He shot a nervous glance at Kincaid, who was pouring beer onto Red Beard's face to put out the fire smoldering in his whiskers. Hardare said, "It was you, wasn't it? You ripped them up."

"Not all of them," he stammered, and with a trembling hand extracted a badly creased snapshot from his pocket. "Here, it's yours. Keep it. Please. Just don't cut me up."

Hardare stared at it. Of the eight photographs Hardare had brought, the biker had chosen to save the youngest one of his daughter, and the only one of her in a bikini.

Hardare punched him squarely in the mouth.

* * *

The victory party back at Kincaid's ranch was a somber affair. Hardare had bruised a knuckle, and to keep the swelling down was soaking it in a bowl of ice. In the next room he heard Jan and Kincaid mumbling to themselves as they studied the hundred-dollar drawing of Santa Maria prison.

"I'm going to get a soda," Jan said loud enough for him to hear. "Either of you heroes need another beer?"

"I can always use another beer," he heard Kincaid say.

"No, thanks," Hardare told her.

The beer was kept in the garage, and when they heard the back door slam Kincaid said, "Something keeps bothering me. Tanner said the locks in Santa Maria were different. Will you use different lockpicks to open them?"

"Probably."

"How will you know which ones to bring?"

"I won't. I'll have to bring a whole kit."

"I figure there are at least eight locks to get through. Is that going to slow you down?"

"Yes," he admitted.

"How many minutes? Give me a ballpark figure."

He shrugged. "Say fifteen."

"No." Kincaid walked abruptly into the living room. "Tell me you're kidding," he said.

"Look, this is difficult work," Hardare said, not liking the storm in the man's eyes. "It's not something I can rush."

"Maybe you'd better learn. I've broken into three

171

prisons in my life. Two in Nam, one in El Salvador. In Nam we blew off the locks—real John Wayne stuff— and in El Salvador we just stole the keys and ran through the joint. My limited experience tells me we can't spend more than nine or ten minutes inside Santa Maria in all."

Jan walked into the living room with two opened bottles of Lone Star. She handed Kincaid one, swigged her own.

"A few years ago, I saw you escape from Alcatraz," Kincaid said, now standing over him. "It took less than five minutes. Why should Santa Maria take any longer?"

"Because Alcatraz was a publicity stunt," Hardare said, realizing how bad the words sounded the moment they came out.

"You mean it was a hoax?" Kincaid said.

"No, it was real," he said, "but it was planned in advance. A few days before the escape, I visited the prison to inspect the cells. Actually I was checking the locks to know which lockpicks to bring. On the day of the escape, I had the picks hidden on me."

"What if they hadn't let you inspect the cells?" Kincaid said almost before he'd finished speaking.

"If it's an old jail, it doesn't matter. The locks are usually unsophisticated. If the jail is newer I sometimes back out."

"How many times have you done that?" Kincaid said.

Hardare stood up and several ice cubes escaped from the bowl. "Look, you told me Santa Maria was old. Old prisons are usually cakewalks. I didn't expect there to be several different series of locks. These things

172

aren't easy. Unlike Houdini, I can't just walk into a prison, and walk out a minute later."

Kincaid practically jumped into the air. "Wait a minute! Houdini could have, but you can't? What are you talking about?"

"People assume Houdini taught my father all his secrets," Hardare said, "and that he in turn passed them on to me. Well, Houdini gave my father most of his act, but not all of it. Houdini once made a full-grown elephant vanish at the New York Hippodrome, and my father never learned how it was done.

"Houdini could walk into any jail, be incarcerated, and free himself in minutes. He once escaped from Death Row in Boston City Prison, opened twenty other cells, and switched the other inmates around. And he did it without any preparation."

Kincaid acted confused. "But could he possibly know which lockpicks to bring?"

"I don't honestly know. No one does. I suppose that is why he's still a legend."

Jan spoke for the first time. "Did Houdini have the secret of his escape buried with him?"

"He willed it to a mentalist named Joseph Dunninger. Joe kept it in a safety deposit box in Brooklyn for forty years, then donated it to the Houdini Museum in Canada at Niagara Falls. The secret is kept in a locked box on display, although the security is pretty light . . ." His words trailed off and then, very slowly, Hardare began to smile. "We could fly up tonight, be back tomorrow night. Who knows? Stealing it might be good practice."

Kincaid still had not taken a sip of his beer. "It

sounds like a great idea. Except you don't just run into a museum and rob a display. You have to have a plan."

"Fine," Hardare said. "We'll come up with one on the plane."

Jan shook her head. "You can't be serious."

Hardare stared at them. "Either of you have a better idea?" he said.

A few minutes later Jan was on the telephone making reservations with Continental Airlines for the several connecting flights that would take them to Buffalo, New York, later that night.

Chapter 12

The Houdini Secret

S hivering from the cold spray, Jan and Hardare stood huddled together on an observation platform overlooking Niagara Falls. It was a bleak, dispiriting morning, with only a handful of bundled tourists to watch the roaring spectacle. While they waited for Kincaid to return with the rental car, Hardare fed two quarters into a pay telescope and watched Jan play tourist.

Coming back to the Falls had depressed him. He had nearly made a small fortune here, only to see it slip away. This was in the mid-seventies, the decade of gullibility, when audiences were willing to pay Muhammad Ali four million dollars to run away for fifteen rounds from a pseudo-Japanese wrestler, and later shell out another six million to see Evel Knievel bail out before his jet rocket ever made it to the other side of Snake River Canyon.

"This is sensational," Jan said. "Here, take a look."

He stood immobile, hands warming in pockets. "No thanks."

"You act very unimpressed. How chic."

"This place makes me sad," he said. "A long time ago I thought I could be the first man to ride the Falls inside a barrel. I rehearsed for an entire month one summer. Then I had to scratch the entire thing."

"Let me guess." She swiveled the telescope in his direction. "You sobered up."

"Found out it had been done before."

"No."

"By a woman."

"—the kiss of death."

"Mrs. Anna Edson Taylor. She woke up one morning, kissed her husband, and climbed inside a pork barrel stuffed with pillows and took the big plunge."

Out in the street a car horn blared. It was Kincaid, looking cold and impatient behind the wheel of a blue Ford Taurus. Locking arms, Jan and Hardare fought a gust of wind to reach the curb, and climbed into the front seat. Kincaid handed them both cheap pairs of drugstore sunglasses and wool pullover hats, then in an irritated voice said, "You two stopped squabbling yet?"

"I thought that was how married couples were

supposed to act," Jan replied. "This car is freezing, Frank."

"Our Budget car has a budget heater," Kincaid said, pulling down the street. "It doesn't work."

The Houdini Museum was located on Centre Street only a few short blocks away. Earlier Kincaid had cased it, and as he maneuvered the car down the twisting streets and avoided pedestrians more concerned with the cold than traffic signs, he gave them his impressions. There was an internal alarm system, which he assumed was wired to the police station. There was also a French Canadian guard, old, smelly, with a hearing aid and the hots for a pimply girl selling tickets at the door. The only real obstacle was the "Houdini Secret" itself, which was encased in a thick glass box on a display pedestal. The glass had to be broken, and that meant making a racket. Luckily the display was not in a prominent spot, and obviously had more historical than monetary value. So long as they stuck to the plan and moved quickly, Kincaid did not foresee any problems.

Centre Street had two museums, one erected to Hardare's uncle, the other to Robert Ripley, whose "Believe it or Not" cartoons had made him a household name. Kincaid had his pick of parking spaces, and as they got out he pulled a peaked cap over his ears. The soldier was dressed like a hick on a bus tour, a disguise he considered necessary since he would be sitting in the car with the engine running, and visible to anyone who walked by. Unlocking the trunk, Kincaid removed a collapsible baby carriage and quickly assembled it on the street.

"I never thought I'd be pushing one of these," Jan said.

Opening his red flannel jacket, Kincaid removed a pouch filled with burglar tools and put it into the carriage. He had brought everything but plastic explosives, which he had not wanted to risk smuggling over the border when they'd driven into Canada from the Buffalo airport late the night before.

They stood huddling across the street from the museum. A few tourists went out, but none went in. It was a slow day, another plus. Kincaid said, "I'm going to park the car on the corner near the drugstore." He slapped Hardare on the back. "Ready to break the law, buddy?"

Hardare didn't have a good answer. Despite the cold, he was perspiring heavily beneath his warm argyle sweater. The closer he came to actually breaking the law, the more disoriented and conspicuous he felt.

"Come on, *dear*," Jan said, pushing the carriage ahead.

Hardare locked arms with her, and together they crossed the street. It felt odd pushing a stroller again, especially with a woman he didn't know, nor particularly care for. At the curb he gently lifted the carriage onto the sidewalk.

The museum's façade was a replica of an old vaudeville house. It had a smoked glass entrance and splashy billboards announcing the never-before-seen wonders on display inside. Admission was $5.00 for adults, $2.50 for children under the age of 12, senior citizens accompanied by their parents, free. The gag was so old that Jan laughed. Hardare bought two tickets.

"Don't be nervous," she said reassuringly, as they

pushed the carriage through the swinging glass doors. "By the time they know it's gone, we'll be safely back at the hotel."

"If it was that easy," he whispered, "someone would have already stolen it."

An elderly guard with a hearing aid tore their tickets in half. He smiled brightly at Jan, then at Hardare.

"You sure make a nice couple," he said as they passed.

Hardare hadn't been inside the museum in years. Along with Houdini's most famous illusions and escapes, the museum used old sepia-tone photographs to tell the story of his uncle's life. On one wall he saw a photo of Houdini with Hardare's father, on another, one of his mother holding hands with Houdini's wife Bess. It was no different than opening up an old family album.

A horde of chattering Japanese tourists were ahead of them, and Jan hung back, looking without interest at a series of photos circa 1900. As the Japanese lingered around the legendary "Water Torture Cell," Jan pointed at a particular photo and said, "Who's this man? Your uncle acts like he wants to kiss him." Hardare took a look; it was Harry Day, dressed in black pants with spats, a white shirt with the sleeves rolled up, suspenders, and a pork pie hat tilted rakishly on his head. He was smiling like a recent millionaire. Houdini stood beside him, his right arm slung affectionately over Day's shoulder, the sun brightening his big smile. In every-

179

one's life there should be a person like Harry Day, Hardare thought.

"My uncle went to London in 1900," he said quietly. "He was convinced he had to gain recognition in Europe before he could make it in the States. For a while nobody would book him. He ran out of money, and actually had to steal to feed himself and his wife. Then one day he met Harry Day, and everything changed."

"Was he an agent?"

"No, a publicist." He pointed at a photograph of Houdini preparing to jump handcuffed into a river. Day, beaming brightly, stood in back. "Day knew the importance of working with newspapers. That was the key to getting publicity. He concocted a scheme for Houdini to be locked in handcuffs by the superintendant of Scotland Yard. If he could escape from the policeman's cuffs, Day figured, every newspaper in London would write him up. If he couldn't, Day said he'd buy him two steamship tickets back home." They moved down the hall, Hardare pointing at a photograph of Houdini in manacles at Scotland Yard. "My uncle agreed. I guess he figured at that point he had nothing to lose."

Jan said, "Was he allowed to inspect the handcuffs?"

"No—and I'm sure it worried him. He wasn't familiar with English jails. Many of the locks were dated and strange to him."

"So he just said to hell with it and did it anyway?"

"Something like that. Day got hold of several newspapermen he was friendly with, and they descended on Scotland Yard. The superintendent on duty had been forewarned and gave Houdini a thorough frisk. Then he pulled out a pair of the oldest handcuffs my uncle had ever seen." He found a photograph of the inspector snapping the ancient pair on Houdini's extended wrists. Jan studied the fading scene intensely. "They were called 'darbies,' and my uncle just wasn't familiar with them. He also thought they were rusty."

"He looks scared to death in this picture," Jan said. "What did he do, back out?"

"I think he wanted to, but Day was talking so much he didn't have a chance. Then the superintendent really dug the knife in. Instead of putting my uncle in a room, where he could sit and study the darbies, he led Houdini outside to a courtyard, took the cuffs off, made Houdini put his arms around a huge pole, and relocked his arms as tightly as possible."

The Japanese horde was gone. Jan motioned him down the darkened hallway. In a whisper she said, "You wouldn't be telling me this if he didn't escape."

"You're right."

They passed the "Water Torture Cell." "How?" said Jan.

"Nobody really knows," Hardare replied. "His biographers claim that he banged the darbies against the pole, and because they were old they opened themselves. But my father was certain my uncle used a special pick."

"What do you think?"

"Houdini never left anything to chance. He must have had a hair-thin pick palmed in his hand. How he happened to know which pick to bring is beyond me."

"And why we're here," Jan said.

They passed "Walking Through a Brick Wall," the "Milk Can Escape" that had nearly cost Vincent's father his life, the "Vanishing Elephant" (no explanation included), the "East Indian Needle Trick," and a display of handcuffs and leg irons before reaching the glass-enclosed shrine that housed the "Houdini Secret."

It wasn't much to look at. An antique oak box sat on a black carpeted pedestal. A printed legend hung on the wall behind it:

THE HOUDINI SECRET

This box contains six wooden boxes within it. The seven boxes diminish in size, and the final box is thus protected by the locks of the six boxes that contain it. That Houdini used picks, keys, springs, and other contrivances for his escapes, is a self-evident fact. How he was able to pick the right key for the right lock at the right time, however, when there are over 8,000 varieties of lock mechanisms, is a mystery the solution of which is forever concealed at the heart of these boxes, and it will forever remain a mystery.

"You're sure this is for real?" Jan said.

"The answer is in there. I know that."

"I hope so." She took the pouch from the baby carriage, removing a mallet and can of adhesive spray.

Shaking the can, she sprayed the glass display, waited ten seconds, then brought the mallet down swiftly. There was a muffled noise. Half of the case cracked and fell in glistening diamonds to the floor. Hardare put his hands on the box, felt its weight. "Hold it," Jan warned. She removed a rock the size of a baseball from the pouch and tossed it to him. "On the count of three, I pick up the box, you put down the rock. Ready?"

He brushed a shard of glass off the top of the box. "Ready."

"Okay. One, two . . . three."

She lifted the box and Hardare adroitly replaced it with the rock. The alarm hidden in the ceiling remained silent. Jan placed the box into the baby carriage and covered it with a small blanket. Locking her arm into his, they pushed the carriage through the museum's twisting corridors.

"What do you think we should name him?" she said.

"Harry," Hardare replied, keeping his eyes peeled.

They passed the final exhibit—"Anna Eva Fay's Spirit Cabinet"—and Hardare breathed a sigh of relief. They were back in the museum lobby, and through the smoky glass doors he could see the rental car parked on the corner with its engine running.

They pushed the carriage into the lobby, and Jan froze, suddenly noticing the electronic anti-shoplifting box beside the entrance they had just passed through. "Damn," she swore as a wailing alarm sounded throughout the museum.

Jan tried the front door, found it locked. Taking the box from the carriage, she tossed it to him. Then she took the mallet and banged out the glass in the doors. "You first," she said, standing aside so he could jump through. Ducking his head, Hardare leapt through the gaping hole, and the moment Jan had joined him, took off running.

Cradling the "Houdini Secret" in his arms, Hardare ran in a cold, punishing wind, the piercing wail of a police siren less than a few blocks away. For the first time Hardare realized that police sirens weren't meant just to clear traffic; they also instilled a sense of fear and desperation. With a burst of adrenalin, he flew into the front seat of the idling rental car.

"Where the hell is Jan?" Kincaid said, gripping the wheel.

"*What?*" Hardare said breathlessly. He turned completely around: back at the front door Jan lay face down on the sidewalk, the museum's white-haired security guard holding her firmly.

"Wait here," he shouted at Kincaid, pulling his wool cap down over his ears as he jumped out of the car.

"No!" protested the white-haired guard as Hardare returned. He released his grip on Jan and slowly stood up. "I'm unarmed. Don't hurt me."

"Get out of my way," Hardare told him, hearing the sirens draw closer.

The white-haired guard heard them also, and put his foot against Jan's back, forcing her back down. "What's wrong with you people?" he said indignantly.

"A great man's life is depicted here. You have no right stealing an exhibit."

From the car Kincaid yelled, "Get rid of him!"

Using his right hand only, Hardare grabbed the guard by the lapels of his leather jacket and cleanly lifted him off the pavement and into the air. Jan scurried out from beneath him, then stood up, gaping. Hardare let the guard fall, and he landed with a *whumph* on the seat of his pants.

They jumped into the car and Kincaid sped away. After a confusing series of turns he stopped unexpectedly at a red light. There were no other cars in sight, and Hardare's right foot pressed an imaginary accelerator. "Never run if nobody's chasing you," Kincaid had said when he had mapped out the robbery that morning. Good advice, until the light changed, and a police car came speeding down a one-way street and began to ride their bumper. When Kincaid did not pull over, the police car deliberately rear-ended them, and continued to jostle their car the length of the block, while up ahead Hardare saw two more police cars forming a roadblock.

"Want to see a great trick?" Kincaid said. He took a black metal egg from his pocket, ripped the pin in it with his teeth, and drove the rental car directly at the roadblock's center. The egg flew out the window.

"Hold your ears!"

The egg detonated in front of them and Hardare held his head in agony. The policeman standing in front of the cars went to their knees, and Kincaid accelerated through their roadblock, knocking the cars aside. By the next block, Hardare felt his hearing return.

"What was that? A miniature atomic bomb?"

"German stun grenade," Kincaid said, looking into his mirror. "Makes a hell of a bang without hurting anybody. I usually carry a couple around for laughs. We've still got company."

The first police car had stopped momentarily at the roadblock, and seeing no one seriously hurt, immediately continued to pursue the fleeing trio. Kincaid took a hard left, and Hardare heard the rear bumper fall off their car. The police car tried to follow; crossing the double yellow line, it crashed head-on into a lime green Nova going the opposite way. The Nova spun like a top, jumped onto a sidewalk, and uprooted a mailbox, while the police car plowed into the rear of a parked taxi. Screaming an unintelligible denunciation out his open window, Kincaid gunned the rental and quickly left the scene.

Five minutes later he dropped Jan and Vincent off in the Holiday Inn parking lot. "I'm going to dump this heap. See you in the room."

"Someone must have seen our license," Hardare said. "The police will contact Budget and trace the car to you."

"Come on! You think I used a license and credit card with my own name on it?"

This struck Kincaid as very funny and he drove off laughing. Hardare gave Jan a tired smile. She was covered with gravel and dirt, her blouse was torn, and her hair looked like a disheveled rat's nest.

"How's Harry?" Jan asked, smiling back.

Hardare clutched the box to his chest. "He's fine."

They went inside the motel.

* * *

Logan had heard Kincaid's shout clearly; Kincaid had rolled down his window, and called out, "Maggot fuckheads!" at the two battered men in the green Nova.

Logan did not think his nose was broken. He held a blood-soaked Kleenex to his nostrils, and with his thumb and forefinger gently felt the bridge. It hurt, but not severely. His face had hit the steering wheel just hard enough to give him a good nosebleed. He glanced at Dorsey beside him, holding the sleeve of his jacket to his forehead.

"I thought you said you weren't hurt," Logan said.

"I'm not," Dorsey mumbled. "We've got company."

One of the policemen in the car that had hit them head on was tapping his knuckle against Logan's window. Logan rolled it down and in a weak voice said, "Yes, officer?"

The policeman crouched down, staring inside. "Are either of you seriously hurt? Any bones broken?"

"I'm fine," Logan said, "but my friend smacked his head against the dashboard. He says he's having problems seeing. I think he has a concussion."

The policeman grimaced. "Just stay right here. I'll call an ambulance." He got in his car. His partner was sitting behind the wheel holding a wadded handkerchief beneath his swollen left eye.

"One of them is badly hurt. We'd better call an ambulance."

His partner used the car radio to make the call. When he was done, the first policeman went back to the Nova.

The two men were gone.

No room in a Holiday Inn had ever looked so good.

Hardare lay face-up on one of the beds and tried to calm down. His heart was still pounding, he could hear it, and his mouth tasted like a dirt road. He'd worked under pressure before, but that was on stage or before a camera, in a controlled environment. What he'd just gone through was definitely in the wild.

"I'm ringing room service for lunch," Jan called from the adjoining bedroom. "What do you want on your burger?"

"Tomato, no onions. And medium rare." If anything had surprised him this morning, it was watching Jan in action. The robbery and car chase hadn't fazed her, and he wondered if working with Kincaid had conditioned her to being in dangerous situations. Still, he had to admire her nerve.

Jan came into the bedroom he was sharing with Kincaid. It was small, with a TV bolted to the wall, two single beds, a round plastic table, two chairs, and a print of a painting of Van Gogh's sunflowers nailed to the wall. The "Houdini Secret" sat on the table, and she lifted it with both hands. "This is heavy. How many boxes inside?"

"Six."

"You've got your work cut out for you."

Getting up, Hardare took a Cross pen-and-pencil set from the bedside table, unscrewed them, and removed a thin set of lockpicks from their hollow interiors. "Is that part of the trade?" Jan asked.

He said nothing. His tools: six ultra-thin tungsten steel lockpicks that he always carried. Usually he was not so dependent on his props, but an incident in Monte Carlo had taught him the need to always be prepared.

He had been working in the floor show of a swank casino called Le Mirage. It was a good time in his life; his wife was alive then, his daughter young and traveling with them, and he was earning more money than any other variety act in Europe. One night between shows he went into the lobby to make a phone call. When he was finished, he pulled at the door of the small booth, only to find it locked from the outside. Someone, probably a dancer in the show or a drunk, was playing a practical joke on him.

He had searched his pockets for something to open the door with. He had nothing on him, not even a plastic credit card. That left him two options.

The first was to rap loudly against the glass, and attract a passer-by's attention. But, the odds were good that he'd be recognized and would look like a fool.

That made his second choice inevitable. Putting his shoulder to the door, he jammed his heel against the wall, and snapped the door's hinges. Then he made a fast exit to his dressing room, and imagined that in a dark corner someone was having a good laugh at his expense.

Never again, he'd told himself at the time. The most important thing he had was his reputation. Having the lockpicks made had been his wife's idea. Most men carried monogrammed handkerchiefs; he would have customized burglar tools.

"That box looks too ordinary to be something Houdini once owned," Jan said from the other chair.

He examined the lockplate with a penlight. "It looks ordinary. Which usually means—" he played with the plate, and it shifted to one side to reveal three hidden keyholes "—it isn't ordinary at all."

"What is that?"

"It's called a puzzle lock. A German locksmith invented them about a hundred years ago. They used to be considered impossible to open without the key. Knowing Houdini, the five boxes inside are a matching set, with each box being progressively harder to open. This might take a while." He stuck a pick into one of the keyholes. Nothing happened.

"Why not break it open?" Jan suggested.

He shook his head. "If I don't have the skill to open them, what good is Houdini's secret going to do me?"

She bit her lip. "I don't mean to sound pessimistic, but what if you can't open them all?"

"Then we take the box back to the museum," he said, testing another pick.

Twenty minutes later Jan brought a tray of food into his room and set it beside him. It was the all-American meal: a juicy hamburger, cottage fries, cole slaw, dill pickles, and a diet Coke. He glanced up from his work. "I'm not really hungry."

"You shouldn't work on an empty stomach."

Smothering the hamburger with ketchup, he took an inhuman bite, and went back to work. He ate without thinking, his mind absorbed with the intricate puzzle lock, and before he knew it the hamburger was gone.

"Do you mind?" Jan asked, looking over his shoulder. "I won't be offended if you want to be left alone."

"Pull up a chair. I can use the support."

Ten minutes later the first lock yielded to his ability and clicked open. He lifted the lid and removed the smaller box within. It was an exact replica of the first, although its finish had not aged as severely, and he examined the lock intently.

"I never realized how much skill it takes to be proficient at what you do," Jan said, smoking a cigarette. She made eye contact with him, smiled. "Do you mind if I ask you a question?"

Sometime in the last hour she had brushed her hair out and put on jeans and a navy cashmere sweater, and Hardare found himself becoming increasingly distracted. "It doesn't cost anything to ask," he said.

She laughed. "All right. Do you mind telling me how you levitated the guard?"

"What are you talking about?"

She lit up another cigarette and gave him a hard stare. "The museum guard who nearly knocked me cold. You appeared to lift him clear off the ground with one hand. I've never seen that trick before."

Hardare gave her a bemused grin. "Really? Would you like to know how it was done?" Jan nodded, and he pointed to the bicep in his right arm. "Feel it," he said, turning his right hand into a fist. A questioning look crossed her face: she gave the muscle a powerful squeeze, and offered a thin smile.

"I never realized you were so . . . strong."

"It's the only life insurance I have," he said.

"I once read that Houdini was unbelievably strong," she said, "but always assumed it was a myth."

"Not at all. When Houdini was a young man, he met a circus strongman named Emil Jarrow. Jarrow was smaller than Houdini, yet twice as strong. In exchange for sleight-of-hand lessons, Jarrow helped Houdini get into perfect physical condition."

"How," Jan asked. "Lifting weights?"

"A little bit. But also a great deal of calisthenics, running, and strengthening of the lower back. In one of Jarrow's exercises, you must hold a fifty-pound dumbbell straight out to the side with one hand, while your other hand writes your name repeatedly on a chalkboard. The exercise doesn't build muscle, but it does make you stronger."

Jan shook her head. "You certainly had me fooled." She stood up. "Maybe we can talk later, after you've learned your uncle's secret."

"I was planning to show it to you."

Her eyes widened in surprise. "You were?"

"You nearly got arrested for helping me steal this. I'd be pretty ungrateful if I didn't share it with you."

"That's . . . very nice of you." Jan went to the door and unlatched the chain. "I'm going downstairs to buy a paper. Frank should be back soon. Good luck with the locks."

She left before he could reply. Maybe we can talk later. He considered it, decided it might be a good idea. Then he quickly put her out of his mind, and resumed his work. Outside a firehouse whistle blew. It was noon.

A half hour later he stopped. Two more boxes had yielded to his abilities, and he felt pleased with his progress. Glancing out the window he saw giant flakes of snow falling onto the streets. The sun had died out.

He went into the bathroom and peeled off his clothes. With the opening of each lock much of his old technique was returning. His father had spent years teaching him Houdini's methods, and lately he'd been getting sloppy. Picking locks was like playing a piano; without constant practice, the memory lost much of what it had learned.

The shower's blasting spray jolted him awake. During his travels he'd spent countless nights in hotel rooms, and one of his idiosyncracies was to use whatever free toiletries the hotel offered. Herbal-formulated shampoo, Neutragena soap, scented body rinse—he spread them over his body, rinsed, and used two downy towels to dry off. The shower had invigorated him and he felt happier than he had in months. He was pushing himself again. Jan seemed to like the man she saw in him. So, finally, did he.

He slipped into fresh clothes. The connecting door to Jan's room was cracked open and he peered in. Empty. He decided not to worry about it. He sat back down at the table. His watch read *12:40*. With three boxes remaining, he set a time limit; he'd be finished by one-thirty. It would be hard, but not impossible. He took a deep breath and started in.

Within twenty minutes he had mastered two more boxes, but his elation was short-lived.

The last box was painted jet black, and had one of the most complicated locks he'd ever seen. He stuck a pick into the keyhole and blindly plunged ahead.

Ten minutes of work got him absolutely nowhere. The lock's mechanism followed no discernible pattern and he became exasperated. He'd tried every method he knew and even a few variations. What now?

He picked up the last box, holding it above his head so the light shone through the keyhole. The box had a strange feel, and by applying pressure with his palms, he moved the sides up and down. Very slowly the box came apart in his hands.

Hardare wanted to let out an elated yell. Finally it made sense to him. It was a puzzle box, and not just in the mechanical sense. The key to opening it was a test of ingenuity. He had assumed the last box would be the hardest to open, when in fact it was the easiest.

He glanced at his watch. It read *1:28*.

Inside the box were two objects, a large drawstring bag and a sealed yellow envelope. He placed both delicately on the table.

He opened the envelope first. The wax seal was his uncle's—he recognized the fancy *H.H.* imprint—and he gently slitted it. Inside he found eight pages of Houdini's own handwritten instructions and pencil sketches. They were dated November 29, 1916, almost ten years before Houdini's untimely death.

Normally, he would have read the instructions, and

not experimented with the secret until he understood its principles. But his curiosity was too great, and he put the papers aside, excitedly undoing the drawstring bag.

Inside he found a cracked leather belt. It was very wide, like a money belt, and nearly three quarters of an inch thick. It was also heavy. Examining it, he found that it contained a double wall, a belt within a belt. Sucking in his stomach, he put it around his waist. It fit perfectly.

The belt had a strange feel around his midsection, as if it contained a life of its own. Each time he breathed, it moved a fraction, and he touched the cracked leather gingerly and felt tiny hidden ball bearings.

What had he found? By exerting the slightest pressure with his forearm, he could make the inner belt move invisibly around his waist. All it took was a feathery touch.

The inner belt was designed to be moved back in forth in front of a spectator's eyes without the motion being detected.

It was genius, and he snatched the notes off the table. This belt, Houdini stated in the opening paragraph, was the result of a lifetime of experimentation and work, designed to open any mechanical restraint or lock ever made.

Or any prison in the world.

The hotel did not have a magazine stand, and Jan braved the frigid cold and walked down the street to buy a copy of *USA TODAY*. Of the six instructors at

Kincaid's Anti-Terrorist Training School, Jan believed she was the only one in whom Frank had confided the secrets that could be learned by reading the classifieds in the nation's largest national paper. Only a week before she had found a CIA "message," and although it had said nothing that Kincaid did not already know, her ability to discover it had still drawn Kincaid's highest praise.

She had to wait in line—a woman with a pronounced New York accent had bought a map, and demanded that the cashier show her how to use it—and she glanced at the headlines, noticing with an odd satisfaction the tremendous amount of both political and civil unrest here, and abroad. Bad times, as Kincaid often reminded her, were the best times for business.

When she came out of the stationery store, it was snowing hard. Pulling her sweater up beneath her chin, she scurried back to the Holiday Inn, her boots slipping on the icy pavement. Halfway down the block she heard steps, and spun around expecting to see Kincaid behind her. "That's odd," she muttered. There was no one there.

The Holiday Inn was a warm refuge, and she went to the bank of elevators and pushed a button. A hand touched her shoulder.

She turned. Kincaid stared at her sullenly, his peaked cap dotted with snowflakes. "Where have you been?" she said.

"Up on the fucking roof."

"Doing what?"

"Watching you being tailed."

Jan's cheeks grew flush. She had let her guard down, and could sense her teacher's keen disappointment. "I'm sorry, Frank," she said after a moment's hesitation. "I didn't think anyone knew we were in Niagara Falls."

He placed his icy gloved forefinger against her nose. "I'm not paying you to think. Or to drool over Hardare."

"Drool over Hardare? What are you—!"

"Save it. Last night, when you thought Hardare and I were both asleep on the plane, I watched you. Your eyes never left his face. Didn't you hear my stomach growling?"

The elevator doors opened and he said, "Let's go up."

Jan got in and Kincaid pushed the penthouse button. "I only walked one block," Jan said. "How did you spot the tail?"

"The asshole got out of his car without his hat on. He also stayed the exact same distance behind you. Not normal."

"Any idea who he is?" Jan said.

"I don't know. Who do *you* think he is?"

She thought about it for several floors. "You mentioned two men tailing you at the Brownsville airport. Said you spotted them by the way they were dressed. I would think he was one of them."

"And you would be right," Kincaid said. The elevator settled into the penthouse and the doors parted. They went down a short hallway and Kincaid put his shoulder to a heavy metal door that led onto the roof. They went outside into the blinding snowstorm that had suddenly enveloped the entire Niagara Falls area.

They were nine stories up and Jan held his arm, feeling completely at the mercy of the gusting wind. Kincaid pointed an accusing finger downward. Canvassing the street, she quickly spotted the only parked car with its engine idling.

"But *who* are they?" she said.

"A pair of CIA maggots. I think they take orders from the man who hired us."

"Which means?"

"He doesn't trust us. Or isn't telling us something."

Bending over, Kincaid scraped up snow in his gloves and packed it into a ball. When it was of suitable size he gave it a tremendous hurl, and the sound of its deadening impact on a car roof below only reinforced to Jan why she loved working for Kincaid. She saw two men, both without hats, get out of a car.

"My god, Frank," she said. "You cracked their windshield."

"I want you to listen to me," he said solemnly. "You and I and Vince are what people in the government called 'expendable operatives.' People who can be used in dangerous situations who, if caught, can't be traced. The only protection we have is our own ability to stay alive. You reading me?"

Jan nodded. "Loud and clear."

The raging storm had turned him into a snowman and he wiped a wet mustache from his upper lip. "I want you on your toes at all times. No more lapses. And no more drooling."

"I wasn't drooling."

He jerked open the metal door. Warm air brushed their faces. "You left the hotel without your jacket. Why? Because you thought you'd be back in a minute? Do you remember the first lesson I ever taught you? Or didn't it sink in?"

"Prepare for the worst."

"And you didn't. Your mind was elsewhere. Okay, that's all."

By now the cold was making her shiver uncontrollably. She pictured Hardare in her mind and decided that for the moment he wasn't worth losing her job over. Inside the elevator Kincaid removed his hunting jacket and draped it over her shoulders. She looked at the puddled floor and mumbled a faint thanks. He hit the button marked "Four."

They got off on their floor. Kincaid rapped three times on the door of their room, waited, knocked again. Unlocking the door, they went in and simultaneously searched the adjoining bedrooms. Kincaid came into Jan's bedroom holding the last empty box of the "Houdini Secret" in his hands.

"Vince's gone," he said. "We're fucked."

When Hardare hadn't returned three hours later, Kincaid called Continental Airlines and made reservations for two to Brownsville for the first available flight out. He hung up and Jan said, "We can't strand him here, Frank."

"If he doesn't turn up in another hour, we're going to have to. The only thing I can think of is the police traced us, came up here, and arrested him. If they've got brains—or if they make him talk—they'll be back pronto. No sense in the three of us going to jail."

"I don't like it," Jan said, sounding frustrated, sitting on her bed, the phone book open at her feet. "We called the hospital, the police, the airlines to see if he made a reservation on a flight out. Nothing. He's not anywhere. One minute he's here, the next he's gone."

"I don't like it, either."

Kincaid's expression became taut, his entire body stiffening. He turned to face the door. Jan stared, gasping: dripping melting snow, his hair plastered to his forehead, Hardare stood in the narrow foyer, his soaking wet shoes forming two dark spots on the carpeted floor. He grinned at them oddly, like someone out of his mind, or on drugs.

"How long have you been standing there?" Kincaid said quietly.

"Not long," Hardare said. "Maybe a few seconds. I let myself in."

"How did you get a key to Jan's room?" Kincaid asked suspiciously.

"I didn't," Hardare said, still grinning. "I don't need a key anymore."

Kincaid and Jan stood and listened to him tell about the "Houdini Secret." He was like a child with a new toy. He could walk into any building, any home, any store, anywhere he wished to go, effortlessly. He told them he felt transcended, lifted to a new level of his own profession. "Let me show you," he said excitedly, dragging them out of the hotel into the storm. "I know the perfect place."

The perfect place was a greasy spoon named Niagara Coffee and Doughnuts, only two blocks away. There were more cockroaches scurrying across the linoleum floors than there were customers and they slipped into a booth facing a twisting cobblestone street lined with specialty shops. The stores closed at three, then opened again at four-thirty, Hardare explained. It was now four twenty-five. He decided to order coffee first, and killed another minute waiting for their waitress, an ancient specimen working in slow-motion. They ordered, and Jan requested tea and clean silverware, thank you. Their waitress scowled.

"Maybe if we leave food on the floor the bugs won't attack us," Jan suggested.

"I didn't come here to eat." Hardare pointed out the frosty picture window. "I'm going to take a quick walk up the block. Jan, I want you to time me."

Removing his Rolex, he showed her how to activate the stopwatch mechanism, then slid out of the booth and went outside. He walked in a brisk but relaxed manner, blowing repeatedly in his bare hands. Kincaid pressed his face to the window.

As instructed, Jan hit the timer when Hardare reached the opposite curb. The first shop on the street was a French bakery, and he stopped fleetingly at the front door, then hurried to the next shop, which sold vulgar T-shirts and Niagara Falls souvenirs of every imaginable description. Here he repeated his actions at the door. He did this from shop to shop, flowing effortlessly down the empty sidewalk, his momentum building.

At the far corner he crossed, and worked his way back toward them, his hair growing white with snow. As he drew closer, they noticed that he was talking to himself.

"He's flipped out," Kincaid mumbled disapprovingly.

His face aglow, Hardare entered the diner at the precise moment their waitress appeared with their hot drinks.

"I beat you," he said, sliding in beside Jan. Shaking the snow from his hair, he said, "How long?"

"One minute, thirty-two seconds," Jan said.

"Fantastic." He sipped his coffee.

"You just did a great imitation of someone walking down the street," Kincaid growled, not touching his cup. "So what?"

"I just committed twenty-two acts of presumed illegal entry," he replied. "Take a look for yourself."

A Niagara Falls city bus had stopped in front of the diner, a group of local merchants and bundled-up shop girls getting off. It was a loud, friendly group, and as they exchanged good-byes and went to work, Hardare put his nose to the window, wondering who would be the first to discover his tampering. The baker? The bookstore owner? It was a foot race.

The jeweler, a wiry man with a pinched face, had the fastest legs, and let out an exaggerated cry the moment he reached his store. "Help! I've been burglarized! Someone call the police!"

Two doors down, the baker found his shop open, and joined the jeweler's lament. "They've broken into my store too! Help!"

Within seconds, the rest of the store owners had formed a chorus, and the scene bordered on the absurd. Each merchant had something to say, and like a bad opera they filled the street and yelled simultaneously. All they need is a fat lady, Hardare thought.

When no fat lady appeared, a policeman who didn't look old enough to shave came huffing around the corner. The merchants swarmed around him, and he quickly pieced the facts together, and made a door-to-door search. Every shop was unlocked, yet nothing seemed to be stolen. He shook his head in bewilderment. What was the crime if there was no breaking and no entering?

"Twenty," Kincaid counted. "Twenty-one. Twenty-two."

"But that isn't possible," Jan said almost in exasperation. "Not in one and a half minutes?"

Kincaid leaned across the table and squeezed Hardare's shoulder. "Congratulations. You hit paydirt."

Their check came and Hardare dug out his wallet. "I'm still learning. When I get comfortable with the 'Houdini Secret' I'll move much faster."

Chapter 13

One A.M.

*I*t was past midnight when Jan, Kincaid, and Hardare arrived at Brownsville International Airport, claimed their bags, and took a taxi to Kincaid's ranch twenty-five miles north in Olmito.

The moon was full, and the shadows it created in the uneven road kept their driver guessing, his foot repeatedly hitting the brakes to avoid a coyote or frozen jackrabbit imprisoned between the headlights. In the distance they could see a house so brillantly lit up that it was visible for miles. Turning a familiar corner, Hardare suddenly realized where he was, and that the radiant home was actually Kincaid's ranch.

"Looks like someone's having a party," the owner growled.

The taxi skidded down the gravel front drive and dropped them off at the front door. They took their bags and went in. Kincaid stole silently through the downstairs, and in the living room found his Spanish houseboy sound asleep on the sofa with a double-barreled shotgun cradled in his lap.

Kincaid cautiously took away the gun, then awoke him with a snap of the fingers. His houseboy jumped up with a start, blinking his eyes wildly, and began to babble non-stop in Spanish. Although Hardare had a good command of the language, he could only decipher a few key words of the boy's coarse slang.

"Pedro thought we had some intruders," Kincaid explained. He went to the fireplace and remounted the shotgun. "When he went outside, he found a few coyotes, took a few shots at them. Then he came in and fell asleep. I think we scared him."

While Kincaid spoke, Pedro gathered up their luggage and trudged upstairs to the bedrooms. Kincaid disappeared into the kitchen, returned with three longneck bottles of Lone Star.

"Here's to a successful trip." He handed them each a bottle, then raised his. "And to getting your kid safely out of jail."

They clinked their bottles in a toast, and Hardare added, "Soon," and then took a long icy swallow.

Kincaid waited until Hardare had gone to bed before he decided to investigate. He turned out the lights
in the living room and stared out the windows toward
the distant highway. The coyotes that Pedro had
thought he'd heard weren't coyotes—Kincaid had spotted their tire tracks in the taxi's headlights an hour
ago—and he had to assume they would be coming back
once the house turned dark. He took the shotgun down
from the mantel, and stole silently out the kitchen back
door. Walking around back to the garage, he hopped
on Pedro's mud-caked Moped, pedaled until the engine
kicked in, and drove with the wind to his back across
the bumpy field and out to the highway.

He parked the Moped fifty yards from his driveway
behind a mound of dirt that overlooked his ranch and
the road. Then he sat down in the dirt and waited,
forcing his tired eyes to stay open.

After fifteen minutes he was longing for a Lucky
Strike. He felt for a pack in his windbreaker, then
thought better of it, and popped a stick of gum in his
mouth instead. There was a stiff wind, and anyone with
a good nose would catch the scent of a cigarette from a
hundred yards.

He worked the gum hard. It soon grew tasteless
and he spit it out. Suddenly a jackrabbit darted out from
a bush, its hind legs sending up tiny clouds of dust.
Zigzagging across the field, it disappeared down a hole,
and left Kincaid wondering how long it had been watching him. Probably since he'd first parked the bike. More

evidence that the rabbits and coyotes on his land knew what guns were, and hid accordingly.

The rays of the headlights appeared well before the car. Kincaid watched it slow down at his driveway, his fingers clenched around the butt of the shotgun. When the car started to turn into his ranch, he jumped on the Moped, and without turning on his headlight sped across the field.

He got ten yards behind the car before the driver spotted him. Holding the shotgun with his right hand, he aimed at the right rear tire and fired. The car flew sideways off the driveway, accelerating, and abruptly came to a crashing halt. One of the rear doors opened, and Richard Lyons staggered out.

Kincaid parked the Moped and went around to inspect the damage. The car had run into a gigantic tree stump, the only one left on his property since the land had been cleared. Its headlights were smashed, the bumper ripped clean off. Sitting in front were two men, both stunned, faces banged and bloodied, the same poor slobs he'd sent into an accident back in Niagara Falls.

"You goddamned maniac," Lyons sputtered, leaning against the car trying to clear his head. "You could have killed us."

"Could have, if I wanted to." Kincaid poked his head into the driver's open window. "Hi, guys. We keep running into each other so often, I thought we should meet formally."

He waved the shotgun a few inches from their noses. Their faces registered a mixture of pain and fear. "I've got a boy up in the hills watching you. Stay here, change your tire. I'll be bringing your boss back in a little while." To Lyons he said, "Let's take a walk, Richard. Toward the house."

"What for? . . . Where are we going?"

Kincaid had him by the shirt, and shoved him ahead, using the shotgun as a friendly persuader. "It's time we had a little talk."

Lyons protested and was silenced by a kick in the pants.

"Cut it out!"

"I'm in a bad mood," Kincaid said. "Don't make it worse."

Goosing him with the shotgun, Kincaid goaded Lyons around the house and into the tin-roofed garage in back. As Lyons fumbled with the light switch beside the door, Kincaid slapped his hand away.

"You are the most inept undercover man I've ever met," Kincaid said, taking a Coleman lantern from the wall. He lit the lantern on the lowest flame and hung it back up on a peg. "I sometimes find it hard to believe that I trained you, Richie."

"Not everyone can be an Eagle Scout, Sarge."

Leaning the shotgun against the wall, Kincaid lit up a long-awaited cigarette. "Remember how in Nam I used to keep scoresheets? Each time someone fucked up, it got written down. I guess the exercise was lost on you. I've run out of fingers and toes trying to keep count. Now you have the balls to come *here*."

Lyons tried to speak but Kincaid did not let him. "Listen to me, goddamnit! You're just smart enough to stay in your job, and maybe get a few more promotions. That frightens me, Richie, so I want you to walk out of here remembering two things. First, you have got to learn the difference between a soldier and an undercover agent."

"And what is that?"

"A soldier's life is expendable, while an undercover agent's life is not, *and is never meant to be*. You put two of your men on my tail. Me, a *mercenary*. In my own backyard. That's like forcing them to run blindfolded across a minefield. You should know better."

Again Lyons tried to speak, and Kincaid said, "The second one has to do with trust. For two years you and I and eighteen other righteous dudes ate together, slept together, and killed together. I trusted the men in my unit more than my family back home. *We all did*. When you stepped out of the jungle and put on your pinstripe suit, did you suddenly forget that?"

Silence. Staring at the floor, Lyons expression turned sad, then reflective. Then he said, "I didn't forget. In fact, it's why I risked coming over here. We have a major league problem, Frank. I tried to get a message to you in Niagara Falls without alerting Hardare, but you kept destroying my men's cars."

Kincaid crushed out his cigarette. "What kind of problem?"

"Yesterday afternoon a street kid delivered a message to the U.S. Embassy in Mexico City. The women on duty had enough common sense to fax the message to Washington, and they sent it to the deciphering center in Langley. The message was from Maria Alvarez. It was written in a code used by nightclub mind-reading acts."

"You mean Hardare's kid helped her?"

"Exactly." He lifted his gaze, and in the flickering light managed to look Kincaid in the eyes. "Maria gave us the the flight number and date for Rafael Guerra's next shipment of drugs."

"That was pretty fucking stupid."

Lyons nodded in agreement. "She put herself—and Hardare's kid—in tremendous danger. I don't know if I told you this, but she has a personal vendetta against Guerra."

More bad news. Kincaid said, "You still haven't told me what the problem is."

"This shipment will be the largest Guerra has ever attempted. An entire plane's worth. The government has decided that they can't let it slip in, even if it means jeopardizing one of their agent's lives."

"You mean they're going to confiscate the plane and arrest everyone in spitting distance," Kincaid said.

"Precisely. Once the plane lands on U.S. soil, we impound it. When that happens, we have to assume Guerra will be alerted, and will immediately grab Maria and Crystal so he has something to bargain with once we catch up with him."

Kincaid paused as the largest rat he'd ever seen scurried across the garage floor. He instinctively reached for his shotgun and saw Lyons stiffen. He relaxed his arm. "Which leaves us with the sixty-four thousand dollar question. When does this plane land on U.S. soil?"

"Wednesday," Lyons said. "The flight's scheduled time of arrival is ten-forty in the evening."

Wednesday was the day after tomorrow. Kincaid said, "And if we're not ready by then, you've been instructed to tell me that the rescue is called off."

211

"That's right, Sarge."

"That's just beautiful."

"I have to have an answer."

"Tonight?"

The light from the Coleman lantern grew dim, then died altogether. Lyons couldn't see Kincaid. He said, "You know if Hardare's ready. And you know if you're ready. I need an answer right now, Frank."

Kincaid did not answer him. Lyons waited a full minute, and when his patience was gone said, "Goddamnit, Frank. Hey!"

The jarring sensation of Kincaid's shotgun being dug into the seat of his pants and lifting him up to his very toes caused Lyons to spread his arms out wide, as if preparing to soar up into the rafters.

"Very good," Lyons said, his voice a mere squeak. "I never heard you come around me."

"It was easy. You're as thin as a dime and just as cheap," Kincaid said, jamming the steel barrel forcefully upward. "I don't like the way you play this game. You manipulate everyone around you, then deny responsibility when something goes wrong. To answer your question, yes, Hardare is ready. And so am I. We'll stage the break-in Wednesday night."

"Are you sure you're ready?" Lyons asked.

"I'm sure." Kincaid goaded him with a sharp jab of the barrel. "Richie, take off your clothes."

"What are you talking about?" Lyons nearly cried.

Kincaid tapped his skull lightly. "No back talk. Take off your shirt and pants before I start leaving scars."

Sputtering obscenities to himself, Lyons peeled off his clothes until he was standing in nothing but his underwear. Kincaid led him to the garage door and said,

212

"I think it's time you learned a little humility, Richie. Do me a favor. Tell the two guys who work for you that I apologize for the crap I put them through. Tell them I know they were just doing their job."

"Oh go fuck yourself, Frank," Lyons said, and as Kincaid stood in the doorway and lit another cigarette, hobbled painfully across the gravel driveway to his car.

Hardare sat on his bed, thinking.

It had happened innocently enough. A twelve-year-old boy with blonde spiked hair had come up to him on the airplane, asking for an autograph. Hardare had looked for a piece of paper to write on, and the boy had said, "No, on my shirt," and turning around, shown him the scene stenciled on the back of his white T-shirt. A vicious shark was inches from biting down on a swimming man's head—his own head, Hardare realized. He had written his name in bold script.

"My dad says you're the luckiest man alive," the boy said, and then had gone back to his seat to watch the movie.

Minutes later Hardare had broken out into a cold sweat, and gone into the lavatory to wash his hands. In the mirror, his face looked bloodless. Slapping water on his cheeks, he tried to bring back some color. Above his lip was a tiny cut he had suffered during the shark escape. The doctor at the hospital had said he would probably have a small but permanent scar.

Back in his seat he had tried to sleep. When that didn't work, he'd mimicked Kincaid and had several beers. That only made him feel worse. Jan and Kincaid had both gotten blankets and were sleeping, and he thought several times of waking one of them up, just to have someone to talk to.

Now, hearing footsteps in the upstairs hallway, Hardare got up from the bed, and bumped into Jan in the hallway. "What are you doing up?" he said. "It's nearly two."

"I thought I heard someone outside." Jan said. "I suppose I should ask you the same question."

"I couldn't sleep," he said. Then, much to her surprise, he motioned her into his bedroom. "Come here, I want to show you something."

"I can't. Frank forbids his instructors from going into clients' bedrooms," she said, standing in the doorway.

"Rules are sometimes made to be broken," Hardare insisted, taking her hand, and leading her into the spacious room. The bed was still made, and from the bedside table he took a thick black leather belt and placed it into Jan's hands.

"What is it?" she asked, weighing it in her palms.

"Houdini's secret."

"Really?" She turned it over twice. "Will you show me?"

"I thought you couldn't stay."

"I changed my mind."

Hardare carefully secured the belt around her thin waist. "The belt has another hidden belt inside. The inner belt is fastened to tiny ball bearings. By using your elbow, you can make the inner belt travel in a complete circle around your waist."

Jan moved the inner belt with her elbow. "That's amazing. I can feel it move, but I can't see it."

214

"The inner belt has ten compartments. Each holds twelve different lockpicks." He opened a flap on the front of the belt. "One hundred and twenty picks in all. Each exactly the same length, three and a half inches."

He took a pick out and placed it on her outstretched hand. It was hair thin but unusually pliable, made from tungsten steel. Jan turned it over on her palm, peering intently in the semi-darkness at Houdini's hand-crafted masterpiece.

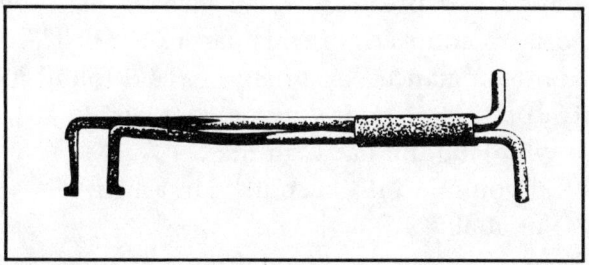

"To open a lock," he said, "you need a pick and a wrench. The wrench puts pressure on the cylinder, the pick lifts the tumblers. Houdini developed this special pick—in his notes he calls it a "universal"—to cut down the number of picks he needed. With one universal, I can open a dozen different locks."

"And the belt holds a hundred and twenty?"

He nodded. "They're arranged alphabetically and each slot is coded. Under *B* you find picks for Bramah locks, British two-lever and three-lever locks, Bottleneck handcuffs, and so on. There's a pick for practically every lock made."

"This is fantastic. With your ability you can walk in and out of Santa Maria in a few minutes."

"Let's hope so," he said quietly. Sitting on the bed, he removed a universal from the belt, and began to meticulously clean away the years of accumulated dirt with a patch of cloth. Jan sat down beside him, watching intently.

"How many do you have left to go?" she asked after a minute.

"I'm on the C's right now," he said.

"You'll be cleaning all night."

"Probably."

On the bedspread Jan spied a small, rusty key. She picked it up and said, "Is this part of the belt?"

Hardeen glanced up briefly. "Yes. I found it in an empty compartment. It's just a standard key. I don't know why Houdini had it in the belt."

"Do you mind if I keep it?" Jan asked.

"Not at all."

Removing a silver chain from her neck, Jan unclasped it, and slid the rusted key onto the chain so it hung next to her St. Christopher's medallion. "Is this the only reason you asked me in here?" she asked, slipping the chain beneath her cotton shirt.

"No," he said, still polishing.

Her hand touched his wrist. "There's something wrong, isn't there? You don't sound the same."

He nodded. Then he took a deep breath, wondering if he could explain. "I once knew a tightrope walker named Karl Wallenda. Karl used to perform with his family. For a finale, they made a human pyramid three tiers high. It was a great act, until one of them slipped. Two of Karl's sons died. Karl healed, and went back to walking, but he wasn't the same. One night we had dinner, and he mentioned his fear of falling three times.

I knew then he would kill himself on the wire. He knew it too."

"Did he?"

"Six months later, doing an outdoor walk in San Juan. I saw it on television. It was windy, and when he fell he screamed. I've seen people hurt in the circus before, and I saw a man killed on a trapeze, but Karl was the only one who screamed."

"What does that have to do with you?" Jan said after a moment's hesitation. "Why should you be afraid of anything? You escaped from the sharks, didn't you?"

"I discovered a few years ago that saving your own life is a hell of a lot easier than saving someone else's," Hardare said.

"I don't understand what you mean," she said.

"You don't? Well, I guess you and Kincaid didn't do your homework. It was in all the newspapers." He slipped the universal lockpick back into its proper slot in the belt. "Two years ago, I let my wife die in a car accident. I've spent my whole life showing people how brave I am, and the one time it really matters, the one time it counts, I chickened out."

"How did it happen?"

He took another deep breath. "We were driving into New York City on the Long Island Expressway. I was going fast, hit an oil slick. The car skidded, did a somersault onto the grass. I was thrown through the windshield, got up as the car caught fire. I ran, saw Barbara through the shattered windshield. She was unconscious, still strapped in. If I shot my arm in, I could grab her shoulder. She was right *there*."

"But . . ."

"I didn't," he whispered fiercely. He got up from

217

the bed, went to the window, gazed out. "I couldn't move. Frozen to the spot. It was a reaction I had never encountered before. Then the flames leaped up. She was gone in an instant." He snapped his fingers. "Just like that."

Jan moved to stand beside him. "I'm so sorry," she said.

"For a long time I had a hard time facing myself in the mirror," he said, the words now flowing. "No one blamed me for what happened, not even Crystal, but I couldn't stop blaming myself. I suddenly knew how Karl had felt. Like him, I started to think about failure constantly. As a result, I had to junk half my act. The hard stuff. That's when I stopped getting booked in Vegas, and I once co-headlined there. So I moved to London. The agents weren't as demanding and I usually got work. Of course my salaries died." He shook his head miserably. "I nearly ruined myself."

"Deciding to rescue your daughter must have been terribly difficult," Jan said.

"Yes and no," he said. "I have to have her back. And I guess I saw it as a chance to redeem myself. Except I also knew I could screw up. That I could kill my daughter, as well as my wife."

"You're not going to fail," she said firmly.

Hardare shrugged. "I don't know. Every time I think I have it conquered, I see Karl's face. Once Karl lost his boys, he was cursed."

"You think you're going to die, don't you?" Jan asked, suddenly understanding. "Well, if this is any consolation, Frank certainly doesn't, because he wouldn't go into that prison with you if he did. And neither would I."

"Thank you," he said without conviction.

"Vince . . . You can't change what happened to your wife. And you've got to stop worrying about your daughter. It will only ruin your chances to free her."

"I wish I knew how," he said.

Standing on her tiptoes, Jan kissed him on the lips. "Maybe I can help," she said.

An hour later, in bed, he touched her and said, "I haven't felt this good in a long time."

"Rules were made to be broken," she said, kissing his neck.

Chapter 14

The Vanishing Elephant

Dawn invaded the fields, its golden rays climbing up the sides of the house, creeping through the windows, touching the headboard and then settling resolutely on Kincaid's face. He awoke instantly and sat up in the twisted sheets, his eyes canvassing the room. Four years of sleeping in rice paddies and all-night firefights had instilled in him an habitual alertness, and he awoke every morning at dawn, even if he'd gotten riotously drunk the night before. A doctor had diagnosed it as "Charley Paranoia," and said it would stay with him long after his combat memories were forgotten. He lived with it.

Getting out of bed, he stretched his stiff muscles, then went down on the hardwood floor and did a hundred perfect pushups. The last ten were a real struggle—black dots clouded his eyes—and he forced them out, fighting his own advancing years the way he fought any other adversary.

Finished, he stood slowly, feeling the heady rush. In Nam he had smoked pot, even some opiated hashish, but the high was nothing compared to the feel of his own blood pumping. He went into the bathroom and took a hot shower.

He was out of shaving cream, and lathered his beard with soap and scalding water. He wasn't good at keeping house, or keeping his house staff in line, and there was always some essential they were out of. It would be six years April since his wife had died of multiple sclerosis, and the house, *her* house, still felt unsettled to him, as if the furniture wasn't just right, or the colors were not matched.

Throwing on a robe, he padded downstairs. Pedro had fixed coffee, and he poured a mug full and sauntered onto the back patio. Blue skies and a cool wind greeted him, and he took in several deep, satisfying breaths, tasting it like good food.

He walked off the patio into the prairie grass. His ranch encompassed two hundred acres, and the richness of the rolling hills was the purest definition of beauty he'd ever known. Sometimes, when no one was around, he'd throw on his combat fatigues and boots and race like living hell across it. First up a steep hill behind the garage, then down the lagoon through a natural path the wind parted for him in the knee-high grass. Then he'd turn east where the field opened up, smooth and flat and unchanging. Running, his thoughts turned subliminal: a petrified bone, a tuft of burned grass, they seemed as important as any idea rattling around in his head. In the distance he'd see the house, and pretend a sniper had him in his sights. His feet would practically leave the ground.

Not today; no time for it. He went inside, refilled his mug, and sat at the kitchen table, laying out Tanner's hand-drawn map before him. The map, and bits of information Lyons had given him, had let Kincaid form a good mental picture of the prison's interior. By American standards, it was not a maximum security facility. It was run more like a work farm, and the inmates had some freedom of movement. Traffic in and out of the prison moved with similar ease, and he did not see a problem in getting past the front gates in a garbage truck or delivery van.

Inside the prison would be a different story. Although the break-in was intended to be "enemy-friendly," he wasn't walking in unarmed. Only the Peace Corps was stupid enough to enter hostile areas without guns. Prison guards were not the bravest species, and he opted for snub-nosed .38s, which had a lot of bang, Uzis, and hand grenades.

He started a shopping list, adding flashlights, flares, compasses, a First Aid kit with plasma and morphine, and plastic explosives in the unlikely event they found a door Hardare couldn't open. He didn't think he'd missed anything, but still double-checked. He didn't want to be in the middle of a skirmish and discover he'd forgotten to buy bullets.

"You're up early," Hardare said, coming downstairs in his bare feet. He'd already showered and shaved yet still wore a sleepy expression. His face lit up when he saw Tanner's map.

"Help yourself to the coffee," Kincaid said, finishing the list. He re-read it several times, then took the pencil and drew a line through several items that he would be unable to use.

Edging up to the table, Hardare sipped coffee while reading over Kincaid's shoulder. "Why did you cross off so many things?"

"I always write down what I would ideally like to bring on a mission," Kincaid explained, "then hone it down to the important essentials. Which includes traveling light."

"What does this mean?" Hardare asked, pointing to the last crossed-out item on the list. "Armored RV?"

"That's an armored assault vehicle. I was thinking about using one for our getaway."

"An assault vehicle?"

"The one I have in mind would serve us ideally. German-made, very fast, and can climb right up the side of a mountain." Kincaid slid the map closer. "The airport we will be using when we leave Santa Maria is eight miles away. In the assault vehicle, it would only be four miles away."

"How is that possible?"

"Simple. We drive over the mountains instead of using the roads." Kincaid drew the route with his finger. "Four miles as the crow files. It would cut our getaway time in half."

Thinking about it made Hardare excited; if anything

had worried him about the break-in, it was how they would get away without being blown to bits. "Why not use it then? Too expensive?"

"Not really. I even know an arms dealer in Brownsville who has one for sale, or did last week when I called him. The problem is getting it inside the prison. I've given it a lot of thought, and there's just no feasible way."

"Would the assault vehicle fit inside a truck?"

"It would fit inside a small truck, sure," Kincaid said. "What are you thinking of?"

"You told me that most of the prison's food deliveries and garbage pick-ups are made at night," Hardare said. "Can't we pose as delivery people, and hide it inside the truck?"

Kincaid turned in his chair and stared at him as if he'd completely lost his mind. "Excuse me, but has it occurred to you that the prison guards might want to look inside the truck?"

"It has."

"And what do you think their reaction might be when they see what we're carrying?"

Hardare gave him an easy smile. "They won't see it."

"Come again?"

"I said the guards won't see it. I promise."

Kincaid gave him a funny look. "Earth to Vince, come in!"

"Can you get me a truck? I'll be glad to show you."

"You're serious, aren't you?"

The smile vanished from Hardare's face. "Of course."

Four hours later Hardare was ready. He drove up to Kincaid's ranch in a smooth-handling Army surplus jeep painted in green camouflage and honked the horn. Moments later Jan and Kincaid emerged and climbed into the back seat. They sped away.

The ride was too bumpy to do anything but hold on, and they drove in silence to the deserted area in a large field where Hardare had parked the borrowed truck. Beside the truck were two folding metal chairs, and he put the jeep behind them. They got out, and Kincaid said, "I thought magicians needed a big stage to work their illusions on."

"They usually do," Hardare replied, "but this isn't an ordinary illusion. Please be seated." Once they were, he went to the truck, and opened its rear door by vigorously pulling down on a metal chain. Jan and Kincaid stared into the truck's stark interior. Wiping his hands with a handkerchief, Hardare said, "As I've told you, Houdini did not reveal all of his secrets. The one effect that truly perplexed everyone, including my father, was 'The Vanishing Elephant.' In 1918, Houdini appeared at the New York Hippodrome and made a ten-thousand-pound elephant named Jennie disappear. The stage Houdini was working on was above a gigantic swimming pool, so the audience knew Jennie didn't fall through a trap. The cabinet Jennie vanished in was also elevated."

Kincaid interrupted him. "Do you mind if I get a closer look inside the truck? Or do I have to stay here?"

"I only brought the chairs so you would be comfortable," Hardare said. "Feel free to take a closer look."

"Thanks." Removing his sunglasses, Kincaid walked up to the open vehicle and stared intently into its hollow interior. After a moment he shook his head and said, "I know it's gimmicked, but I can't see where. You do good work."

"Thank you." He waited until Kincaid was again seated before continuing. "Houdini appeared at the Hippodrome for nineteen weeks, the longest engagement of his career. If you can believe the newspaper accounts of the day, the trick became the talk of New York, and completely baffled some of the greatest minds of the day. I had many conversations with my father regarding the trick, and he said it was physically impossible for Houdini to have hidden Jennie on that stage. Therefore, it was his belief that Jennie *did not actually disappear*."

Kincaid stared at Jan, then back at Hardare. "Would you mind running that one by us again?"

"Maybe I should give you a demonstration instead. Give me a hand, Frank." Lying on the grass beside the truck was a short metal ramp used for loading heavy objects. The ramp was heavy, but together they managed to secure it to the rear of the truck. Climbing into the jeep, Hardare started the engine, and drove the jeep halfway up the ramp, then stopped. Kincaid, sensing he was standing too close, dutifully sat back down.

"What I'm trying to say," Hardare said, clutching the wheel, "is simply this. In Houdini's day, when a magician said he was going to make something disappear, he actually made that object leave the stage, one way or another. The 'Vanishing Elephant' was based on an entirely different principle. Jennie never went anywhere; the audience only *thought* that she was gone.

"Frank, after I drive into the truck, please lower the door with the chain, and then sit back down. This shouldn't take me more than a minute."

"Whatever you say."

With that, Hardare inched the jeep up the ramp and into the truck's interior. Kincaid closed the rear door, but instead of sitting back down, got down on his knees and climbed underneath the truck. When he emerged a full minute later he was covered with a grimy mixture of black oil and dry red dirt.

"What did you find?" Jan whispered.

"A goddamned oil leak," he said, wiping his blackened palms on the legs of his blue jeans.

"Serves you right for snooping," she said.

From inside the truck they heard Hardare say, "Did you find what you were looking for, Frank?"

"Don't rub it in," Kincaid growled back.

"I'm ready to come out now."

"This had better be good." Taking the chain in both hands, Kincaid yanked down and the rear door flew open. He stared up into Hardare's face, then past him, seeing nothing but an empty space.

Hardare jumped down to the ground. He glanced at Jan, then over at Kincaid. On their lips he saw words forming, yet heard nothing come out. In their faces he saw astonishment and wonder, and instantly knew what they had both looked like as children. It was the moment that magicians live for, no matter how small the audience.

"It gets better," Hardare said. Kneeling down, he

found a small rock. He let Jan and Kincaid have a look at it, then said, "Watch!" and with a flick of his arm tossed it into the truck. They heard the rock bounce across the metal floor and loudly ring against the back wall.

Kincaid's mouth dropped open. "I knew there was a reason why I didn't like you," he said. "I don't suppose there's a chance that you'll tell us how it's done?"

"No," Hardare said, "but I will give you a clue."

Raising his arm, Hardare slowly turned over his right hand. Sitting in the fleshy center of his palm was the rock that he had apparently tossed into the truck. He let the rock drop onto Jan's outstretched hand. She closed her fingers over it and a knowledgeable look spread across her face. "Now I understand. Because we heard the sound of a rock, we thought we saw the rock. But we really didn't. We only imagined we saw it."

"You must have a tape recorder hidden in the truck," Kincaid said. When Hardare nodded, he said, "Let me guess. You're using a voice actuator to turn it on. You showed us the rock, said, "Watch," and made the fake toss. That cued the voice actuator, didn't it?" Kincaid moved closer to the truck. "Watch!" he said, almost shouting.

Moments later they heard a rock bounce across the metal floor and ring loudly against the back wall.

"I love it," Kincaid said. He whacked Hardare enthusiastically on the back and knocked the wind out of him. "I think we're ready to pull this thing off."

Catching his breath, Hardare said, "When?"

"How does Wednesday night sound?"

"You mean tomorrow?"

"I sure do, buddy."

Hardare stared into both their faces. "I think it sounds great," he said without hesitation.

"Glad to hear it. Now how about making my jeep reappear?" Kincaid said. "Or are you going to make us walk?"

Chapter 15

Disappearing
Act

*I*t had been the longest day Hardare could remember, yet now, staring through infrared binoculars at the prison that held his daughter captive, he realized that the day had just begun.

At first, he was reminded of old pictures of the concentration camps. Barbed wire fences, snarling Doberman pinschers, their masters armed with high-powered rifles, patrolling the darkened grounds. Spotlights from the watchtowers scanned Santa Maria's exterior, as if announcing a huge sale. He glanced at his watch for the hundredth time. *Five minutes and counting.*

He handed the binoculars to Kincaid, and climbed down from the passenger seat of the yellow delivery truck. The truck, which contained their armored assault vehicle, had been painted with the logo of a local moving company, which came into the prison once a week to pick up clay pots, quilts, and straw baskets that had been hand crafted by the inmates.

Hardare tasted the cool night air. Less than thirty minutes before he had gotten his first taste of action, and it had not been so bad. Using automatic weapons, he and Kincaid had easily commandeered another prison delivery truck off the highway. The original crew, now chloroformed and bound, were sleeping on the back step of a nearby Pemex station. Along with the crew's papers, he and Kincaid had also borrowed their identification tags, slipping in their own mug shots above the originals. Hardare's fake ID was pinned above his left pocket, and he glanced at it for reassurance. His new name was Diego Fonts and he thought, *you'd better not forget it.*

He walked down the runway to where Jan was standing next to the plane. During the six hours it had taken him and Kincaid to drive the truck from Browns-ville, Jan had flown the Cessna into Mexico City, re-fueled, and then flown here, to a tiny landing strip a few miles from the prison. They had met up an hour ago, and he had hardly a chance to speak with her. "How's it going?" he asked.

"I've never been good at waiting." She glanced at her watch. "Frank said you didn't have any problems going through Customs at the border. You'll have to tell me how that trick works someday."

"When this is over, I probably will." He held her in his arms and kissed her. "How do you like the disguise?"

"You look too refined to be a delivery man."

"Thanks."

"When are you leaving?"

"Soon. Frank is scoping the prison out now. He wants to be sure it's quiet before we go in."

"Vince, there's something I have to tell you," she said.

"Let's talk later, okay?"

"No, we have to talk about it now." There was an urgency in her voice that he had not heard before. She pushed herself away from him and he saw that her eyes were moist. "I know I shouldn't betray Frank, but I can't continue lying to you."

"Lying to me about what?"

"Just listen," she said.

A minute later Hardare heard a low whistle from the cab of the truck. He looked into Jan's eyes. "Why didn't you tell me this before?"

"I don't know. I'm sorry." She removed the chain from around her neck that held her St. Christopher's medallion and Houdini's rusty key. "Please wear it," she said. "It's always brought me luck."

He slipped it on. "I'll take any advantage I can get."

"See you soon," she whispered as he walked away.

Hardare got into the cab and said, "Let's go."

"It's show time," Kincaid said, gunning the engine.

They drove for several miles across twisting mountain roads, then had to descend a steep hill with several blind turns. Kincaid let the truck crawl down the incline.

At the bottom of the hill they rounded a curve, and Santa Maria became plainly visible through their windshield. For the first time Hardare had a good look at the three machine gun turrets in the towers above the barbed wire fences, and realized what an open target they would be if anything went wrong.

"What's your name?" Kincaid barked at him.

"Diego Fonts."

"Next time, say it like you mean it."

They had to pass two checkpoints. Grinding to a halt at the first gate, Kincaid stuck his arm out the window with their papers. A yawning guard emerged from a tiny house and inserted a key into a switch box beside the fence. The gate opened electronically, and Kincaid was in second gear when the guard shouted at them, then walked forward.

"He wants to look inside the truck," Kincaid said under his breath.

"Just do it the way we rehearsed," Hardare said.

They got out and Kincaid spoke to the guard in Spanish, perfectly imitating the coarse accent of the region. Hardare opened the truck's rear door, and the guard shone his flashlight inside. The empty interior was a perfect illusion. The guard seemed satisfied, but as Hardare pulled the chain to close the door, he changed his mind, and decided to climb inside for a closer look. The guard began to hoist himself up, and Hardare glared at Kincaid.

"You'd better not go inside," Kincaid warned him. "There is a family of *rats* inside the truck."

The guard froze, his feet still on the ground. "Rats?"

"*Rats*," Kincaid echoed, this time nearly shouting.

A chorus of rodent squeals filled the truck's interior. The guard took a hurried step backward, shone his flashlight inside again, then shuddered and waved them on. Hardare pulled the chain on the door, and automatically silenced the squeals. He and Kincaid got back into the truck.

Hardare wiped his brow. "That was close."

"That was nothing," Kincaid said, driving ahead.

At the second gate, things went more smoothly. The droopy-eyed guard had seen them talking at the first gate, and he routinely examined their papers and penned his initials on the last page. The gate was raised and the delivery truck rumbled past the forbidding barbed wire.

They were in, and Hardare felt his eyes double in size as he tried to stare at everything at once. It was like being inside a giant fishbowl: lights everywhere, people watching you at all angles, no sense of privacy, no place to hide. He felt the hairs rise on his neck.

To avoid suspicion, Kincaid drove directly to the workshop to pick up their load. The building was adjacent to Building *C*, which faced Building *D* where Crystal was being held. To reach her, they first had to cover some ground, and possibly meet a few guards. "Think of it as crashing a party," Kincaid had said. "Take your sweet time and act like you belong. "We'll blend right in."

Their headlights fell upon forty cardboard boxes. Their load. Parking, Kincaid turned off the lights. He clasped a firm hand on Hardare's shoulder. "Everything you've ever done in your life will seem tame compared to the next ten minutes. Don't mind being scared. It will hone your senses, make everything seem more real."

What a pep talk; fear, breakfast of champions. "I'm not afraid," Hardare said truthfully.

"Don't worry. You will be."

They got out and approached the workshop in the dark. Kneeling, Hardare examined a formidable double door with his flashlight. The lock was a double mechanism that controlled a single dead bolt. "Haven't seen one of these in years," he mumbled, looking for the answer in the belt.

"Trouble?"

Removing two picks, he inserted them into the keyholes and with ambidextrous skill lifted the tumblers. The dead bolt slid free. "Not today."

Inside it was pitch dark. No guards. Their footsteps echoed down the strongly disinfected hallways. Pushing open a swinging door, they entered the basket shop and Kincaid placed his flashlight on a desk so it shone on them. They unzipped their coveralls and stripped down to emerald guard uniforms.

"How do I look?" Hardare asked, smoothing his creased hat.

"About as Mexican as I do," Kincaid said, inspecting. "Fix your tie. Pull your hat down. Remember, if we're stopped, I'm the mouth."

They had argued about this earlier. Hardare's Spanish was too cultivated, Kincaid said, too showy. It would arouse as much suspicion as if he spoke English. Hardare had reluctantly agreed, and promised not to utter a word.

They ran down a hallway, found another swinging door, and shone their flashlights down another darkened corridor. In his jackboots, Hardare felt like a Gestapo agent, and he realized how differently the prison was affecting him from what he'd expected. There was a sense of cruelty here, a harshness to the surroundings that made his skin crawl. And he thought, *it looks so evil when someone you love is being held inside*.

Kincaid glided through the darkened building as if guided by a sixth sense. Hardare stayed at his heels, halting abruptly at a door. "This will take us outside," Kincaid said, testing the knob. "You're up."

Kneeling, he shone his flashlight on the lock, selected a pick, and opened the door without the slightest hesitation.

"I can see the pressure's getting to you," Kincaid said.

Hardare stood up, feeling absolutely euphoric. In the past three days he had tested the belt for hours on end, and not once had it failed him. Each time he experimented with a new pick, he learned a dozen new things about the science of locks, for each pick contained mechanical nuances and special idiosyncracies that the others did not. The belt did not contain one secret but actually hundreds, all waiting to be revealed.

Kincaid cracked the door; they were a stone's throw from Building *D*. An open yard separated them from the entrance, and Kincaid swore under his breath: nowhere for them to hide.

"We'll have to hike it," he said, and had a foot out the door when a pair of guards marched around the corner. Jerking his leg inside, he pulled the door shut. "Lock it," he ordered Hardare. "Christ, make it fast."

Jamming the pick into the keyhole, Hardare re-aligned the tumblers. Seconds later a hand twisted the knob, found it secure, went away. The air rushed out of Hardare's lungs.

"I told you this would be fun," Kincaid said.

Richard Lyons was sitting by the telephone in his suite at the Brownsville Holiday Inn when the door burst open, and Logan and Dorsey spilled into the room.

"Where the hell have you two been?" Lyons said.

Logan sat on the unmade bed, his face masked in fear. "We were at the goddamned airport. I tried to call you ten minutes ago. The line was busy."

"My wife called," Lyons said, seeing the veins pop in Logan's neck. "My daughter has been sick."

"*How did your wife get your phone number?*" Before Lyons could answer, Logan said, "Oh for Christ's sake, just listen. Guerra's drug shipment isn't coming into LAX at ten-forty. The pilot had engine trouble, and landed in Dallas an hour and a half ago. Our guys in L.A. smelled a rat, contacted the Feds in Dallas, and had the plane impounded once it touched down."

Lyons could only manage a loud, "What?"

"Two tons of coke and heroin. Everyone arrested."

"No," Lyons said, rather stupidly.

"By now Guerra has been alerted, and knows we're on to him," Dorsey said, pouring two straight bourbons at the wet bar. "If he's got any brains, he'll get Maria and Hardare's kid out of that prison tonight."

"But how can you be certain Guerra knows?" Lyons said.

"We have to assume that he does," Dorsey said emphatically, handing his partner a plastic cup. Logan gulped the drink down.

"Wait a goddamned minute," Lyons practically spouted. "When I can't be reached, one of you is supposed to assume responsibility." He pointed an accusing finger in Logan's face. "*You* should have aborted the break-in."

"I tried to," Logan said, his eyes watery.

"You did?" Lyons hesitated, fearful. "What happened?"

"I called the embassy in Mexico City. They contacted Kincaid's pilot by radio. She said Hardare and Kincaid had already entered Santa Maria. We missed them by a minute."

Lyons stared into their dullish faces. "What do we do now?"

"We sit it out," Logan replied. He got up, already needing a refill. "Watch a little TV. Pray."

The phone rang. Dorsey placed the receiver against his ear, said nothing. He handed the receiver to Lyons.

"It's for you," he said. "Your wife."

When the guards were gone, Hardare opened the door; the women's cellblock was a stone's throw away. The building was three stories of institutional concrete, the windows black and heavily barred. It had the same gloominess as a mausoleum. Then he and Kincaid stuck their heads outside, staring in opposite directions. They had begun to anticipate each other's actions, and on silent cue went into the yard. They walked briskly, matching each other stride for stride.

With a screech of brakes a, jeep turned the corner, bathing them in its headlights. Hardare remembered the thief's maxim—Don't run unless you're being chased—and he followed Kincaid's example, and slowed to an almost leisurely pace. "Act like you know them," Kincaid said under his breath.

"Right." He waved to the unsuspecting driver, who in turn tooted his horn. The jeep turned at the mess hall, disappearing. They strolled up the front steps of Building *D*, and Hardare opened the door on his first try. Each of the lockpicks in his uncle's belt had been used extensively, and when he put one of them into a lock, it seemed to slide as naturally into the mechanism as the original key.

They entered an empty reception area. They needed to find a guard with an inmate roster, and Hardare examined the door blocking their way to the stairwell. For a moment he stared in disbelief at the lock.

His worst fear: a knob, but no keyhole. Nothing for him to manipulate. The door could only be opened from the other side. A feeling of absolute panic swelled his chest.

"I can't open it, Frank," he said.

"Say what?" Kincaid touched the knob and shook his head resignedly. "Only one thing left to do," he said, removing a pouch of plastic explosives.

"You'll wake up the whole prison."

"No kidding." Kincaid looked at his watch. "You've got ten seconds to come up with a better idea."

"Give me one of your guns," Hardare said grimly after a moment's thought. "A small one."

Kincaid was a walking arsenal. He handed him a pearl-handled two-shot derringer that he kept with the spare change in his pocket. Holding the derringer in his hand, Hardare squeezed his palms together, and made the gun disappear. Then he rapped loudly on the door.

"Jesus Christ!" Kincaid blurted out.

"Shut up and watch."

They heard plodding footsteps. Behind the door a man vilely berated them with a non-stop flow of references to their mothers and grandmothers. A window slid open in the door, and a single bloodshot eye glared at them through the steel mesh.

"Emergency," Hardare said in Spanish. "Open up."

The eye grew wide, blinked once, like a Cyclops. Without warning the door sprung open, and a hulking guard shoved a double-barreled shotgun two inches beneath Hardare's nose.

"You are under arrest you pig-sucking swine," he said in perfect English. "Arms in the air!"

"Brillant idea," Kincaid snorted.

Hardare raised arms in surrender. The guard turned his shotgun on Kincaid. "You," he said. "Do as told. *Now*."

Kincaid complied. The guard glanced at Hardare, and his mouth dropped open. A gun had inexplicably appeared in his prisoner's hands, and was being aimed at his heart.

"I will . . . kill your friend," the guard stuttered, shoving his shotgun point-blank into Kincaid's face.

"Go ahead," said Hardare, and stuck his pistol against the guard's protruding rib cage. "You'll both have a lot to talk about."

The guard began to tremble. With a deft motion, Kincaid took the guard's hand and snapped his wrist straight down. The shotgun clattered to the floor without going off.

"You're real fucking cute," he told Hardare.

They forced the guard into a stairwell with a flickering overhead light. A half-eaten sardine torta and a walkie-talkie occupied the guard's empty chair. A crackling voice barked for attention, and Kincaid picked the walkie-talkie up, putting it to his ear.

"Not for us," he said, relaxing.

Hardare made the guard sit down. "We're looking for two women," he told him in Spanish. "A sixteen-year-old American named Crystal and a Mexican woman named Maria Alvarez." He placed his hand, still holding the derringer, on the guard's shoulder. "The girl is my daughter. Understand?"

The guard gave it serious consideration. "Third floor. Cellblock C, cells three and five."

"Thank you very much," Hardare said.

From his pants pocket Kincaid removed a blackjack and rapped it sharply against the guard's temple. The guard crumpled into an unconscious heap in his chair.

As they started to go up the stairs, Kincaid said, "Who the hell told you about Maria?"

"Who do you think?"

Kincaid gave him an incredulous stare. "Jan. . .?"

"That's right."

Kincaid cursed under his breath, and Hardare said, "At least she's been loyal to one of us."

Jan Black was afraid.

It had been so long since she had felt fear, she had almost forgotten how paralyzing the sensation could be. She, an adrenalin junkie, feeling weak in the knees. She took another deep breath. If she was going to die, she wanted to do so in a calm manner. If there was an afterlife, she saw no point in entering it screaming.

She could still see the fading taillights of Kincaid's truck when the abort call from Mexico City had come in over the plane's radio. She told herself she could still run the truck down, even shoot out a tire, when the unmistakable sound of an approaching helicopter had disrupted her thoughts.

She got out of the Cessna to listen. The chopper was still way behind the mountains, and she had enough time to evaluate her situation and realize it was hopeless. She was sitting in the middle of a very hot Mexican desert. Except for a tin-roofed shack beside the runway, there was nowhere to hide. She could do nothing but stay put, and sweat it out.

A minute later the helicopter passed overhead, its lights canvassing the runway for a place to land. It looked like a piece of military equipment, and when it touched down in a tornado of wind a hundred yards from where she was standing, she saw three men armed with high-powered rifles jump out, and come running toward her. She had expected the police, or even the army, but not three duded-up drug dealers.

Reaching into the plane, Jan grabbed her Uzi. As she began to fire, a bullet whistled past, missing her head and the plane's fuselage by inches. She heard the men's shoes pounding on the runway. Didn't they know how hard it is to shoot and run at the same time?

Crouching beneath the wing, she aimed for the knees, and with three short bursts cut each man down before they could fire another shot. As they fell, she saw each man clearly: two were in their early thirties, one much younger, all mustachioed and wearing silk shirts and layers of gold chains. Earlier, Hardare had said he did not want anyone killed, that it would negate saving his daughter's life, and she wondered if he meant that to include human slime.

The men lay on the runway, screaming. Behind them, the helicopter continued to whirl, the funnels of air it spawned swirling in geometric patterns across the field. The men's screams grew louder. She walked down the runway feeling an odd sense of shame. Shooting them had been too easy; only amateurs made kamikaze runs.

She saw a shadow and froze, feeling the sharp barrel of a gun press against her spine. Where had *he* come from? She dropped the Uzi and thought: *What kind of bastard sacrifices his own men?*

"*Buenas noches, señorita,*" she heard a man's voice say.

Jan felt her throat tighten. Who was he? She turned around slowly, daring to face him. A man as handsome as a movie star was aiming an Uzi like her own at her midsection.

244

Rafael Guerra smiled. "We've been expecting you," he said.

Hardare and Kincaid sprinted up the stairwell to the third floor of Building *D*. The steel door at the top of the stairs had a tricky sliding bolt, and Hardare went to work. In the next few minute he knew he might be killed, and although that scared him, it did not slow him down. Through his mind flashed images of his daughter's reaction; her smile, her tears, her amazement at seeing him. That was what he really wanted, to see that look of total astonishment register in her face.

The bolt slid free. They walked down a short hall. At the hall's end Kincaid peered through a door with a small wire-mesh-covered window. In the next room a guard sat snoozing with a folded Spiderman comic book in his lap. Kincaid silently drew his .38 while Hardare picked the doorlock.

They entered the room on tiptoe. The guard stirred, mumbling in his sleep. Kincaid placed the .38 against the guard's temple, waiting for him to awaken. "For Christ's sake," Hardare whispered, "you can't shoot him. He's asleep."

"I'm open for suggestions," Kincaid said quietly.

Bending over, Hardare untied the guard's shoes, then retied them together. He made Kincaid step back, then slapped the guard in the face with a resounding whack.

The guard awoke with an eruptive snort. Reaching

for his pistol, he tried to stand, and hit the floor with his face. Kincaid felt behind his ear for his pulse. He was out cold.

"You never cease to amaze me," Kincaid said.

Hardare picked the doorlock to Cellblock C. To Kincaid he said, "I want you to stay here."

"And do what?"

Hardare pointed at the stairwell door. "Cover my ass." He grasped Kincaid's shoulder. "Don't worry, Frank. I'll bring your agent out, too. I just want to get my girl myself."

"Hey, it's your show," Kincaid said, consulting his watch. "You've got exactly three minutes."

"Thanks."

"Get moving!"

Hardare entered the darkened cellblock and turned on his flashlight. He could hear women talking in their dreams as he passed each cell. He counted the cells, and at the fifth cell stopped and aimed the flashlight beam inside. There were three cots and assorted heaps of dirty clothes. On the floor was the pair of high-top Nike running shoes that he'd bought for his daughter last Christmas along with a warm-up outfit. He had found her. He stifled the urge to let out a shout.

He examined the lock on his daughter's cell and was surprised by its complexity; it was the first new lock he had found in the prison. He found a pick and inserted it into the keyhole, unaware that in his excitement he was exerting more pressure than was necessary.

The locked refused to yield. He tried again. Nothing. A minute passed. He felt the pick jam and tried forcing it, a beginner's mistake. He heard a spring release and then, unexpectedly, a sickening snap. He jerked the pick out; it had broken in half.

He told himself it was nothing. He fitted the broken pick back inside the belt, found a similar pick, and inserted it into the keyhole. The mechanism refused to yield, and his hands began to tremble. He tried another pick with similar results. Realizing what he had done, he silently cursed himself.

Only one pick in the belt would open this lock, and he had carelessly destroyed it. He began to search his pockets, looking for the pen with the customized lockpicks his wife had given him. He could not find it, and finally it occurred to him where it was—back in the Cessna with his regular clothes.

He gripped the enameled bars to Crystal's cell. Moonlight streamed through a window in the cell and framed her sleeping face. He felt cheated by fate, betrayed, and for a moment felt the overwhelming urge to beat his fists against the bars. He couldn't have come this far . . . for nothing.

He was running out of time. He remembered how Houdini had once opened a cell in London by jamming a skeleton key in the keyhole and painfully banging the lock with his hand. It was a crude method, but what did he have to lose?

He slipped Jan's chain from his neck. The key from the belt was the wrong size, but he shoved it into the keyhole anyway. It was a snug fit, and he cautiously turned it. The lock resisted, and with the palm of his hand he gave the lockplate a hard whack.

Nothing. In desperation he turned the key harder,

and felt something give way inside the lock. *Come on,* he urged himself, whacking the lockplate again. *You're almost there.*

Suddenly the key turned around in Hardare's hand. He removed it with a sinking heart and stared at the jagged piece of metal. The key was too old and had snapped cleanly in half. It was over. He had lost.

Hardare stared into her cell. He wanted to wake her, but knew that would only be torture for her, and for himself. He stared lovingly through the bars at his only child. He had failed to free her, and he supposed that weeks or months from now knowing this would be easier to accept than if he never had tried at all.

Crystal let out a dreamy murmur. He pressed his face between the bars for a final glimpse and felt himself falling forward. He clutched at the bars as the door swung in, unlocked. Unable to keep his balance, Hardare fell clumsily to the floor.

"Who's that?" Crystal said, sitting bolt upright.

Hardare picked himself up, his face and hands covered with dirt. It was not the swashbuckling entrance he had hoped for, but it would do.

"Hey, Crys," he whispered. "It's me."

"Dad? *Dad?*" She leapt out of bed and hugged him uncontrollably. "Oh God, you're really here."

"Hey, shut up," a woman's voice said in English in another cell.

"Shhhhh," Hardare said, holding her. "Throw some clothes on. We've got to move fast."

"Dad, I love you so much."

She jumped into her clothes, and followed her father out of the cell. They went to cellblock three and Hardare's eyes went wide; an absolutely radiant young

Mexican woman, fully dressed, was standing behind the cell door waiting for them.

"I heard you come in," Maria Alvarez explained after he picked the door. She kissed him on the cheek. "Thank you."

"Come on," Hardare said. "We're not out of the woods yet."

Hardare found Kincaid where he'd left him, the sweat pouring down his face. "You're late," he growled.

"I had a little trouble," Hardare said.

"Tell me about it." Kincaid opened the stairwell door and they ran down to the first floor. The walkie-talkie on the guard's empty seat had gone silent, and Kincaid picked it up and shook it. "That's funny." He gave Hardare a cautious stare. "Power's on, but nobody's talking."

"Must be a slow night," Hardare said.

They hurried outside and down the front steps. As Hardare's foot touched the pavement, a man's voice shouted out *"Ahora!"* and the darkened yard was suddenly lit up like a stage. Crystal let out a scream and threw her arms around her father's waist. Reaching for his .38, Kincaid froze and let out a chilling laugh.

"We're history," he said, dropping his arm.

Staring past the jeep's glaring headlights, Hardare saw the shadows of fifty men, each aiming a rifle or pistol in their direction. He tried to act calm. "Do exactly as they tell you," he told his daughter.

She held him and sobbed. "Oh, shit Daddy! *Shit!*"

From behind the headlights emerged a dark-skinned man wearing a blue sports coat. Hardare assumed he was the warden, and in Spanish said, "We'll go with you peacefully."

"I'm sure you will," he replied in perfect English. "Which one of you gentlemen is Vincent Hardare?"

Hardare felt his mouth go dry. "I am."

"Welcome to Santa Maria Penitentiary," the warden said graciously. "We've been expecting you."

Once they had been handcuffed, the warden marched them across the yard with all fifty guards as an escort. As they neared the administration building, Hardare saw their truck parked less than a hundred yards away. To the warden he said, "How did you know who I was?"

"You are a wanted man in this part of the world," the warden answered.

"You mean by the Colombians?" Hardare asked.

"That's right," the warden replied, unlocking the building's side door. "They will pay me a million dollars if I deliver you to them to stand trial."

"I have to be alive to stand trial," Hardare said, his handcuffs clattering to the ground. Shoving two guards aside, he grabbed the warden by the throat. In his empty right hand appeared the derringer. He placed it against the warden's head.

"You are very clever," the warden gasped as the guards surrounded them. "Unfortunately, you have nowhere to go."

Hardare stared into the mouths of fifty rifle barrels. "The five of us are going to walk over to that truck. If your men get any closer, your head comes off. *Comprende?*"

The warden nodded. Much to his surprise, Hardare saw that Crystal had picked open her handcuffs, and was helping Kincaid and Maria open theirs. In a matter of moments everyone was free.

He dragged the warden across the yard. Seeing his chance, Kincaid ran to the truck, opened the rear door, and shoved Maria and his daughter inside.

"You are only delaying the inevitable," the warden said.

Before Hardare could reply, he heard an engine roar, and then a storm of shattering glass. Crashing through the black plywood and mirrors that had disguised it, the armored assault vehicle leapt out of the truck, and bounced on the ground next to where they stood. A metal door on the side of the vehicle sprung open and Kincaid's head popped out. "Room for one more!" he shouted.

"Thanks." Hardare jumped inside, landing in his daughter's arms. Slamming the door, Kincaid put the accelerator to the floor. They lurched ahead as the warden shouted "Fire!"

The bullets sounded like a heavy rain. Hardare threw his arms around his daughter and shut his eyes. As they hit fifth gear, he heard Kincaid shout, "We're going through the front gates. Hold on to something tight!"

Hardare felt the assault vehicle speed up and braced himself for the impact. They went through the gates like they were cardboard. The vehicle was very fast, and when they were safely beyond the prison, he opened his eyes, and stared out the slit of bulletproof glass that served as a rear window.

"They've got four jeeps," he told Kincaid, seeing the warden in the lead jeep. "And a bazooka."

"Let them try to follow us," Kincaid said, driving off the road and straight up the side of a steep hill. Hardare kept his eyes on the jeeps, and after a few tense moments, saw their headlights fade in the distance. He held his daughter tightly as the assault vehicle bounced across the hilly terrain.

"We're almost home," Kincaid announced minutes later. Coming down the side of a hill, he crashed through a fence that surrounded the airport, and drove straight across a barren field. As the Cessna came into view, so did the helicopter parked beside it, and Kincaid hit the brakes hard.

"Come on," Kincaid said, grabbing his Uzi. The four of them climbed out of the assault vehicle and Hardare spent a moment finding his legs. While Kincaid checked the Cessna, Hardare inspected the abandoned helicopter, and found the bodies of three men scattered along the runway.

"Filthy pigs," Maria Alvarez said, kicking dirt in a dead man's face. "These are Guerra's men," she told Kincaid.

"Dad," his daughter said, gripping his arm. "Look."

Hardare followed her stare. At the runway's end sat a dilapidated shack with light streaming through its windows. As Hardare watched, he saw shadows inside, heard voices.

"Bastard must have Jan," Kincaid said. He checked

the ammunition clip on his Uzi. "I'm going in. Stay put."

They watched Kincaid steal down the runway and disappear behind the shack. Hardare held his breath, clutching Crystal by his side. A moment later a single shot rang out.

"That was not Kincaid's gun," Maria said.

"I know," Hardare said anxiously. They were running out of time; he had to do *something*. He made Crystal and Maria get into the Cessna, then took the derringer out of his pocket. As he rubbed his palms together, the small gun seemed to melt away.

"That will never work," Maria said, grabbing the hand in which the gun was palmed. "Guerra is no fool. If he doesn't see both your hands empty he will shoot you."

"Then I'll show him empty hands," Hardare said. Lying across the pilot's seat was Kincaid's pea coat. He put it on, then had Crystal unlace her sneakers. He tied both laces together. In a minute he was ready.

"Both of you stay here," he said. He kissed Crystal on the head. "I'll be right back, honey."

"Oh God, Dad. Be careful."

Maria gripped his arm. "You'll have only one chance. Get him to relax—bring his guard down. You must kill him."

"I know," Hardare said.

He walked uncertainly down the windy runway. All he had to do was walk into the shack, engage Guerra in conversation, get him to momentarily drop his guard—and shoot him. He considered the movements he had to make to secretly get the derringer. If Guerra was watching his hands, it would never work.

You have to distract him, Hardare thought. *Make him watch your left hand, while your right does the dirty work. But how?*

He had no idea. *Try and improvise*, he thought.

Then he stopped, no more than a foot from the door. He identified himself in a clear voice. From inside a man said, "Come in with your arms held high or I'll kill the woman."

Hardare went in. The room had a dirt floor and was lit by a single cobwebbed bulb. Jan sat in the room's center on an upended box. Directly behind her, holding an Uzi submachine gun, was a man dressed more like a playboy than a policeman. He wore a diamond studded Rolex Presidential on his left wrist, a thin platinum band on his right. Against the wall stood an open Cartier overnight bag stuffed to overflowing with U.S. hundred-dollar bills.

"Welcome to the party," Kincaid said dejectedly. He sat on the floor pressing a rag against his bleeding arm.

"You must be Mr. Hardare," Guerra said graciously.

Hardare did not respond. Guerra made a sweeping motion with his Uzi. "Very slowly, open your jacket. Use both hands."

Hardare parted the lapels of the pea coat, revealing his sweat-drenched shirt.

"Pick up the bottom of your coat," Guerra ordered him, "and lift up. Turn completely around."

Holding his jacket up like a skirt, Hardare did a full revolution. "I didn't come to fight," he said, facing him. "I have a proposition for you."

"Really?" Guerra seemed amused. He glanced at

254

his watch. "We have a few minutes before our friends from the prison catch up. First a question."

"Go ahead," Hardare said.

"Something has always bothered me," Guerra said. "The time you jumped from the airplane—were those handcuffs real?"

Hardare did not understand it. Why did everyone ask him that same stupid question? "They were regulation Smith and Wessons," he said.

"So you picked them," Guerra concluded.

"They didn't open themselves."

"No jokes," Guerra said flatly, his voice losing its charm. "What about the sharks? Tell me the truth— there was a secret channel in the swimming pool."

"Every inch of that pool was examined by reporters," Hardare said. *Good Lord—Guerra was a fan!*

"Then how? I want to know."

Hardare hesitated. "Can you keep a secret?"

"Yes . . ."

"So can I."

It took Guerra a moment to comprehend. In anger he fired a round into the ceiling. A cloud of gray plaster fell on Hardare's head, dusting his hair and shoulders.

"Don't dare ridicule me," Guerra said angrily.

"You've got the gun," Hardare replied. He had to sink that home, make him feel in total command. "This is your country—your show. You have Jan, and Kincaid, and me. If I wanted to make fun of you, this wouldn't be the best position to do it in."

Guerra gave him an icy stare. "You like to talk, don't you?"

"Gets me out of a lot of trouble."

"Then why not tell me about the sharks?"

255

"Because I know it fooled you."

Guerra propped the barrel of the Uzi on Jan's chair. "Now I understand. That's what makes you important. Your secrets. Without them, you're nothing."

Just move the gun another inch, Hardare thought. "Something like that."

"Perhaps we can discuss it another time. You had a proposition for me."

"Let my daughter and me go," Hardare said, "and you can keep Maria and these two . . ." Hardare hesitated, feeling Jan's stare. "I will also give you a hundred thousand dollars."

"I don't believe you," Guerra said. He lifted the Uzi and aimed it at him. "This is all bullshit."

Goddamn. It wasn't working. Hardare felt helpless, ready to be slaughtered. He glanced fleetingly at Jan, then Kincaid. He was on his own. "I have the money with me," he said, his voice trembling. "Here. Take it —it's yours. Just don't shoot me."

Guerra's eyes narrowed. "Let me see it."

Hardare reached into his pea coat with his right hand.

"*Stop!*" Guerra shouted, finally moving out from behind Jan. "Use your other hand. Do it slowly."

Hardare dropped his right hand to his side. In slow motion, he cocked his left arm at the elbow, and with his left fingers lifted his lapel, letting Guerra see the lining of his pea coat. Hardare's right hand tensed imperceptibly.

"I don't see anything," Guerra said suspiciously. "What—"

The shot stopped the words. Guerra staggered backwards, his knees buckling, a spot the size of a small pancake staining his silk shirt. It didn't even sound like a gun, Hardare thought, smelling the burned powder. More like a balloon popping or someone bursting a paper bag. It didn't sound loud enough to kill someone.

Hardare fired a second time, sent Guerra reeling back into the wall. The Uzi landed on some yellowed newspapers, and Hardare jumped forward and kicked it away. Guerra slid down the wall until he was sitting, his face still not registering any sign of pain or discomfort, just amazement; the same look Hardare often saw in the front rows of the nightclubs he worked.

"You killed me," Guerra said, sounding like an old man.

Jan leapt out of the chair. "Vince," she cried. "How did you—"

Hardare showed her the piece of shoelace tied to the handle of the derringer. He had run the shoelace through the sleeves of the pea coat, tying the other end around his left wrist. Hardare straightened his left arm, and the gun rode silently up his right sleeve. Bending the arm, he made the derringer reappear in his hand.

A look of appreciation crossed Guerra's face. His lips quivered.

"Very good," he said, closing his eyes.

A minute later they were airborne. Staring down at the hilltops, Hardare saw the jeeps from the prison snaking across the treacherous mountain roads. Leaning back in his seat, he put his arm around Crystal's shoulders, and let the air escape from his lungs. They had won.

When they had reached cruising altitude, Jan put the plane on automatic pilot, and turned in her seat. Touching his knee, she said, "Do you shoot everyone who asks to see how your tricks are done?"

"Not everyone," he said, dropping his hand onto hers.

Epilogue

Two Years Later

From *Variety*   *Thursday, October 8*

The Magic of Hardare
(Caesar's Palace; $25.00 Minimum)

LAS VEGAS, OCT. 7—Magic shows are not usually a hot ticket in Vegas, but management here has made smart choice putting magician/escapologist Hardare into top spot at hotel. Hardare's recent challenge escapes have made him a draw, and in his uncle Harry Houdini's tradition, he manages to pull off a highly entertaining and baffling hour-and-a-half show. There is, to quote the magico's own words "never a calm moment," a boast he lives up to in high fashion.

First half of show is strictly magic and illusions. Although primarily known for getting out of things, Hardare proves no slouch at drawing big gasps. Women float in air, are cut in half, and vanish without a trace. Animals also play a role, and the menagerie includes a flock of doves, a horse, two Bengal tigers, and a 10,000 pound elephant named Jennie that vanishes on a raised platform above the stage. Trick smartly led into show's ten minute intermission.

Second half consisted entirely of escapes. Hardare's presentation, which is tongue-in-cheek but still serious, eventually wins crowd over. He handles his assistants with aplomb, a group which includes the eight Walter Painter Dancers, his eighteen-year-old daughter Crystal, and a looker named Jan. Chemistry works well without getting hokey, and everyone contributes a healthy enthusiasm.

Escapes are still Hardare's selling point, and he works them well. Brand new Buzz Saw escape is good, as is Death by Drowning, but high marks go to finale. Chained inside a car, he is doused with gas, then set afire. He escapes miraculously unharmed.

On night caught, act got standing ovation. Booked indefinitely.

Val.